Acknowledgements:
Many thanks to Vawn Corrigan for her editorial suggestions
and to G.P. Vignoli for his wonderful drawings.
Olivia Connolly

Olivia Connolly

The Incidental Girlfriend

To Dermot
Thanks for the memories

Prologue

Northern Italy, 2020.

It was late morning and the warm spring sunshine flooded the living room with light. I stood at the window looking out at the flowers blooming in the garden under a dazzling, blue sky. There was no noise, not a sound. 'Where are the birds?' I thought. They should have been chirping noisily. It was March and the Italian spring had arrived in all its glory. The avenue outside my apartment was empty. There was no one to be seen. No one passed in front of my window. No housewives returning from the market. No one walking their dog.
My neighbours, like me, were cowering inside their homes, terrified of the silent killer that was lurking outside.
The eerie silence was interrupted by the sudden wail of an ambulance siren. I looked at the clock. Exactly five minutes had passed since the last one. I knew there would soon be another. It was a sound that continued all day and all night. The invisible killer never slept. Only the other day they had come for my neighbour, the alien looking men in the hazmat suits. We all watched from behind closed windows as he was carried down the steps and loaded into the ambulance. We watched in silence, too shocked for tears or prayers. A siren screamed again. Only three minutes this time. My heart felt like lead. Nine hundred dead yesterday, today there would be even more. I was still reeling from what I had seen on the news the previous evening: under the cover of darkness, long lines of military trucks were filmed leaving the hospital, bearing their sad burden of lost souls away from the stricken city that had no more room for them. No more room and no more hope.

I turned away from the window. The spring sunshine seemed to mock us, daring us to go outside. Another siren, another poor soul gasping for breath. I needed something to distract me. I could not bear to turn on the TV with its constant images of overcrowded hospitals and refrigerated trucks filled with coffins.

My phone pinged. It was a message from a friend in Ireland. I received countless messages of comfort from home—little did they know that they too would soon be living the same nightmare. But this message was different. An old friend had written to tell me that the annual festival on Craggy Island had been cancelled due to fears regarding the health crisis. Craggy island! of course! Father Ted! We had often spoken about going together one year to take part in the celebration. This festival takes place once a year on the island where the hugely popular *Father Ted* TV series was made and where fans go to commemorate the memory of the late, great comic actor Dermot Morgan- who played the part of Fr. Ted in the series.

I sat down and stared at the message.

Dermot. My first love. Crazy, wonderful Dermot who had swept me off my feet and into his wild world of comedy and adventure. Almost without realising it, I found my mind slipping away, rolling back through the years to another time, a carefree time filled with love and laughter. I closed my eyes and let the memories take me away.

Chapter 1

The Letter

The letter that would change my life arrived one, ordinary morning. It was August, 1973, and it was a typical, Irish, summer morning. It was grey and drizzly outside, the weatherman the previous evening had said that heavy rain would be interrupted by showers. It didn't bother me much. The kitchen was warm and cosy and there was something comforting about being inside while the raindrops fell against the window in sudden splashes. I loved our kitchen, the pinewood dresser with its cheerful mugs and blue and white plates, the long table with eight chairs with their neatly tied, flowery cushions. The old, farmhouse teapot with the blue cosy that had been knitted by Aunt Mary, always on the go and which poured endless cups of delicious, hot tea all day long.

I was sitting at the table with my Mam, two steaming mugs in front of us. I was telling her about my plan to go to Italy to work as an au pair. She was not impressed.

'*Why would ye want to work as an unpaid skivvy?*' she asked, '*and on the continent—God only knows what could happen to ye over there*', she continued, as if Italy were the heart of Africa or somewhere. '*I saw a filem about them Italians, they all carry knives in their socks*'.

'Even the women?', I asked, 'isn't it too hot for socks most of the time', I added.

'*Don't ye get sarky with me*', she warned. I thought it better not to point out that the only films with Italians she had seen were Mafia films, set in New York.

Luckily, the conversation was interrupted by the sound of the letterbox clattering. I went out into the hall and picked up the letters from the mat. Surprised, I noticed that the first one was addressed to me. I looked at the envelope and saw that it came from Sandymount Highschool where I had sat my Leaving Cert (the school leaving state exam) just two months before. The results weren't due out till the end of the week but my heart started hammering like mad at the prospect of what might be inside.

I wasn't particularly worried as I thought I had done enough to pass but, still, I also knew that I had been anything but a model student. Instead of studying, I had spent most of my time giggling with my friends and honing my stalking skills although it wasn't called that back then. In typical Aries fashion, I had ignored the boys who had shown interest in me and had become obsessed with one, particular, blond-haired boy who had never given me the time of day.

With trembling fingers, I opened the letter. It was from Mr. Canon, the headmaster, known to all the school as Quack, probably due to the fact that he waddled around after his formidable mother all the time.

I read the letter but couldn't quite take in the meaning. It was only after reading it a second time that I realised what it meant. I had received four honours in the Leaving Cert which meant that I had won a scholarship to University College Dublin. Mr. Canon congratulated me on the results and encouraged me to take the scholarship and further my education.

I took the letter into the kitchen where my mother, on seeing my face, immediately jumped to the worst possible conclusion.

'Jesus, Mary and Joseph, who's dead?' she said, clutching her chest. *'It's Paddy, isn't it? I always knew he'd drink himself into an early grave'*. Paddy was one of her three brothers and he certainly knew how to guzzle the Guinness, but then the other two weren't much better.

'No, nothing like that', I answered, 'the Leaving Cert results are out'. Before I could say another word, she launched into one of her monologues:

'Don't tell me you've gone and failed! I knew it! Spendin' all your time swannin' around in them hippy clothes. I'll give ye flower power! I should have walloped ye with a flower pot the first time ye

came home with that leather band around your head. Mother of the seven snotty orphans, what will himself say?'.

'Himself' was my father and a more mild-mannered man you couldn't have met but, for some reason, my mother liked to talk about him as if he were the head of some ruthless drug cartel.

Things moved fast after the initial shock. The plan to work as an au pair went out the window as I found myself really excited at the idea of going to university. I decided to study English and Italian and sent off my application a couple of days after receiving the results. The scholarship covered my fees and books and there was some money for other expenses. The first cheque arrived soon afterwards and I immediately started to think about an outfit for my grand entrance into college life. Despite my mother's scathing remarks, I was determined to continue in my hippy style and the Dandelion market was the place to go.

Chapter 2

The Outfit

I gathered together my best friends from school – the Fab Four- Jan, Trisha and Annemarie to help me choose my new college clothes. We arranged to meet the following Saturday morning under Clery's clock on O'Connell Street, the traditional meeting place for all of us North-siders. Dublin city is divided into two halves, the North side of the river Liffey with its predominantly working class and lower middle-class areas. In short, where people drank tea and spoke in a 'Dublin' accent. To get to the South side, you had to cross the bridge over the river Liffey and you magically found yourself in a more affluent, coffee-drinking area where people spoke with a type of 'posh Dublin' accent.

That particular Saturday morning, the girls and I crossed the bridge and walked past the beautiful Trinity College, the gates of which were the traditional meeting place for all Southsiders. To get to the Dandelion market we had to walk to the top of Grafton Street which was an experience in itself. There were buskers on every corner. They ranged from two small boys singing traditional ballads out of tune, but were so cute that people kept filling their shoe box full of coins, to the long-haired, mournful guitarist singing Donovan songs. We stopped to listen as he was really good and we dropped a fifty-pence coin into his hat. Further on, there was a classical trio playing Bach and after them, a family of traditional musicians playing a gig. People were laughing and dancing in the street, the sun was shining and the American tourists were happily snapping away with their cameras. There was a carnival atmosphere and it was impossible not to be drawn into it. It felt good to be alive. A man handed me a bunch of flowers that he had bought from the stand on the corner:

'For your beautiful curls', he said. Jan spluttered laughing. It was her job to straighten those curls when we went to the disco on Saturday evenings as it was my dream to have long straight hair. It took the poor girl over an hour to get my hair straight and when she finished, she always said:
'Jesus, me arm is hanging off.'
The disco we went to was in Drumcondra which is very close to the city centre and it had the unlikely name of 'The Blind'. It had those strobe lights which made everyone look really tanned, particularly if you wore white, so if we got off with someone, there was always that terrible moment of truth at the end of the evening when the music and lights were turned off and the handsome guy with the sultry, dark skin turned out to be a pasty-faced, pimply geek that we would then have to get away from. The same went for the guys, I suppose, but we girls always went to a lot of trouble and put on loads of make-up while the guys looked as if they had just dunked their heads into a bucket of cold water. It was a terrible disappointment, after we had been grooving to *Superstition* by Stevie Wonder and *Crocodile Rock* by Elton John or smooching to *Touch me in the morning* by Dianna Ross and *Me and Mrs Jones* by Billy Paul, not to mention the unforgettable classic *My ding-a-ling* by Chuck Berry, to have reality hit us in the face and have to find an excuse not to meet them the next evening. The guys were well aware of this risk and always got their request— 'Meet me at the Pictures'—in good and early and well before the lights came on.

Laughing merrily, we continued on our way. At the top of the street there is a small park called St. Stephen's Green and just in front was a small laneway. Down we went and entered another dimension. The Dandelion market was a magical place, a little corner of San Francisco in the heart of Dublin City. As we went in 'California Dreamin'' by the Mamas and Papas came on as if to reinforce this impression. There were multi-coloured stalls everywhere, selling everything from hippy skirts to flowery shirts, long, beaded necklaces to leather bands. There were stalls selling henna and other

exotic oils and the air was dense with the intoxicating smell of patchouli. After much rummaging, I fell in love with a lilac and white uppy-downy skirt—the ones with long handkerchief type ends that were fashionable back then—and a white, gypsy blouse. To complete the outfit, I added the ubiquitous, blue, denim jacket that I wore constantly. I treated myself to a new leather band to wear around my head and keep my unruly, auburn curls in place and as a final touch, I splurged on a new pair of black, double-platform boots. These were a terrible health hazard and were known as coffins as you were very likely to topple off them and get yourself killed in the process. As I travelled on open-backed buses all the time on my merry way round Dublin city and always clambered up the steps to the upper deck, I risked serious injury many times. On one particular occasion, I was coming down the steps when I lost my footing and fell head first down the steps as the bus was turning the corner into Dame Street. I would have fallen straight out into the traffic if it were not for the quick reflexes of the bus conductor who yanked me back by my mop of hair just before I plunged into the street.
'Jaysus, young wan, are ye tryin' to kill yerself? Ye won't get there any quicker if yer dead ye know'.
I didn't answer as I was pretty shaken but even this didn't deter me from wearing the 'coffins' all the time. I was knee high to a grasshopper and had a terrible complex about my height. The coffins added ten inches and made me feel great. I walked tall or more accurately, I stumbled tall, but for me it was worth it.
The girls and I finished our shopping and walked back down Grafton Street to Bewley's Café, the famous coffee shop. We found a table by the window which was a real stroke of luck as we could watch the fun filled scene below. We ordered a pot of tea and four custard slices, our favourites. I had my scholarship money so it was my treat. On the way out I picked up a coffee cake for the Ma, hoping to butter her up so maybe she wouldn't be too scornful about the hippy clothes I had bought.

Chapter 3

The Encounter

The coffee cake didn't really appease the Ma but she limited herself to remarking that I looked like something out of a side show at a circus when she saw me on that fateful morning in September, when I left the house early to catch the bus for my first day at UCD. It was Fresher's week, the introductory week for new students where we would be shown around and introduced to the various support groups that would help us sort out any problems we might have.

I was nervous setting out, I had never imagined myself actually going to university and my stomach was churning when the number ten bus pulled into the campus. I looked around at the other students and felt suddenly a little out of place. Perhaps I should have listened to the Ma after all and worn something a bit more 'respectable'. Most of them were wearing jeans and nondescript jackets and I, in my long multi-coloured hippy skirt, started to feel a little bit foolish. Suddenly the Dandelion market seemed a long way away, perhaps the little corner of San Francisco didn't extend all the way to UCD. But I was not one to be put down so easily. I tossed my curls, adjusted the leather band around my head and wobbled on my high heels after the group of students who seemed to know where they were going. I followed them into a big, glass structure that turned out to be the college canteen and coffee shop.

'Great', I thought, 'just what I need'. I hadn't eaten anything for breakfast as I had been so nervous but now, I was feeling decidedly hungry. I went inside and studied the layout. There were two floors. On the ground floor there was the coffee shop and I looked around with interest. I was comforted to discover that there were many students sitting around, all in various attire. Lots of long-haired youths in flared jeans and flowery shirts—California here I come.

Others were dressed like seminary students with short hair and buttoned up, black shirts.

The girls were equally diverse, some in short skirts and clingy tops, 'ready-come-at' is the expression the Ma would have used, while the majority were wearing the ubiquitous jeans and sweatshirts. I began to relax a little, I wasn't the only hippy present. I had a look at the food on offer: scones, Danish pastries and Club Milks. Feeling I needed some toast to settle my nervy stomach I decided to go down to the canteen which was on the lower floor. Little did I know what a momentous choice this would turn out to be and how the whole course of my university life would be changed by it.

I put my foot on the top step and, somehow, one of the uppy-downy ends of my skirt became entangled in one of the platform heels and there was no saving me as I rolled all the way to the bottom and slammed bang into the legs of a tall, pale-skinned, young man who was waiting to come up. He helped me up and said: 'There's no need to throw yourself at my feet and do you realise that you looked remarkably like a multi-coloured ball as you came hurtling down the stairs?'

The humiliation! I quickly stuffed everything back into my bag, mumbled sorry to the sarcastic wit and thanking him for his help and with as much dignity as I could muster, stalked off to a table. I sat down and tried to collect myself. This certainly wasn't the entrance I had been hoping to make. I picked up a menu from the table and pretended to peruse it, trying to look as if I belonged there. However, the smart arse wasn't finished with me. Over he came and plonked himself down beside me.

'Do you do any other party tricks?' he asked.

I gave him a frosty look.

'It's just that I'm putting on a show and I'm looking for some new talent. I think you'd be perfect for the Truckdriver's sketch. It should take you about twenty minutes to climb up in those boots and that's about the length of the entire sketch'.

The wise guy then introduced himself as Dermot and told me that he was studying English and philosophy and that he was in his final year. He added that he was also a writer and was in the process of putting on a show at the college. The name of the show was Big Gom and the Imbeciles and the name itself should have been warning enough.

I told him that my name was Livvy and that I was studying English and Italian but that I had no acting talent at all and wasn't interested in taking part in the show.

'Well, how about a crowd scene? Could you do that?'

At this point, I just wanted to get rid of him so I said OK, if he needed some people for a crowd scene, I would do it.

'Six o'clock in the English seminar room this evening, then', he said and finally he got up and left.

Of course, I had no intention of going to the seminar room that evening or any other evening for that matter. Still feeling a bit shaken after my fall, I went to the bathroom to splash some cold water on my face. I studied myself in the long mirror. I was grateful for my deep blue eyes and pretty face but that's where my self-satisfaction ended. I hated my tumbling, auburn curls, large breasts and pygmy height but at least I had the coffins to help with that, despite their ever-present risks. Having taken a few deep breaths, I felt steady enough to face the world again.

I took myself off to the library and found a desk in front of the lake- an artificial hole filled with water and swans. I went to the shelves and got some of the books on the gigantic reading list and sat down to read with the best of intentions. I was determined to take my studies seriously and not flitter away my time on boys and fun as I had done at school.

 I was immersed in Emily Bronte when, a couple of hours later, I became aware of some strange noises behind me. I turned around and there was yer man again.

Whispering he said: 'Come on, come and have a drink!'

'I'm studying', I said in my snootiest accent.

'For feck's sake, the courses haven't even started yet! Are you studying to be a nun?'.
'Would you please leave me alone', I said, turning back to my book.
'Ah Jesus, you were more fun when you were doing your impression of a ball', he said and stalked off.

Chapter 4

The Library

The next day I attended the first English lecture in theatre L, the largest of the halls as it held up to five hundred people. It was overflowing with students. They were packed into the seats, sitting on the steps and leaning against the walls. All of us a little in awe of hearing the great man himself as the head of the department usually only spoke on the first day.

The door opened and a tall figure in an academic gown came in and strode up to the dais where the microphone was set up. There was a hushed silence as we all waited to hear the great man speak. You can imagine my reaction when I saw that it was none other than the smart-arse Dermot, who proceeded to give a lecture on some obscure author who was in the habit of writing while on the toilet and who had notoriously campaigned for non-skid toilet paper to be introduced into public toilets. I looked around and saw that some students were guffawing as they had obviously recognised him. I discovered afterwards that his Big Gom shows were very successful and eagerly attended by the students. But some others were listening attentively and even taking notes.

After some minutes the real Head of the department strode in and approached the dais. Dermot didn't skip a beat.

'I'll just hand you over to my assistant here', he said in serious tones. 'I'd like to wish you all the best of luck with your studies'. With that he swept out of the lecture hall to a mixture of raucous laughter and respectful applause.

I'm sure some of those students really thought he was the head of the department and spent countless hours searching for the author with a passion for toilet paper. The Head himself took it in his stride and thanked his illustrious colleague for entertaining us.

From that day on, Dermot began to court me relentlessly. Everywhere I went, he was there. He even managed to convince my Italian professor that he was half Italian and in broken English sobbed to the class about missing his 'omeland'.

He tormented me. I would be at my desk in the library and he would come up to me, throw himself at my feet and in a fake Italian accent and indicating his wrist would say:

'*Look…I cutta my throat forr you. Why you no cam hout wit me?*'

All of this to my tremendous embarrassment and the great amusement of the other students. He would keep it up until he was manhandled out by the porters still shouting:

'*I die forr you*'.

The more Dermot insisted, the more I resisted. I was convinced that he was off-the-wall, bat-shit crazy.

He was a real trickster, always playing some mad character and as he was a superb mimic, lots of people were taken in by him and the joke was usually on me.

One day, I arrived in the library a little later than usual. I could hear the other students whispering and laughing as I approached my desk. I soon saw why…

Dermot had been in before me and had decorated my desk. There was a silk negligée hanging over the back of my chair and a pair of red, lace panties on top of some books. There were two glasses, one of them stained with lipstick next to an empty bottle of champagne. My desk resembled a boudoir after a night of passion. I shoved everything into my bag and tried to get out as quickly as I could. On my way out the door, one of the porters winked at me and said:

'Rough night, huh!'

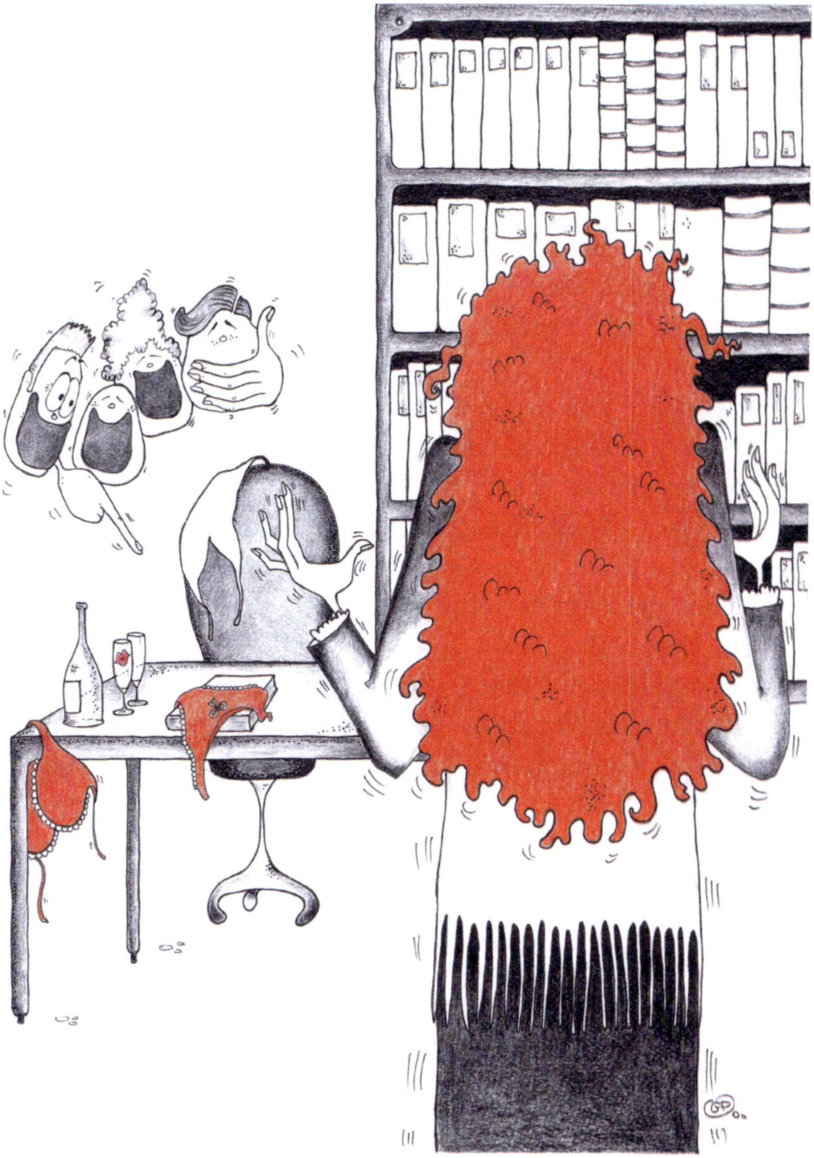

Chapter 5

The Culchie on the Bus

The courtship continued or, more precisely, Dermot's mad pursuit of me went on unabated. I never knew what he was going to do next. Flowers and chocolates were not part of his world as I found out soon enough. I alternated between being exasperated and being amused and attracted too, I have to admit. Although not handsome in the conventional sense, he was very charismatic and impossible to ignore.

I was in the habit of getting the number ten bus that commuted between the city centre and the university campus. As I was still living at home during those first months, the twice daily bus commute was part of my life. In the mornings I would use the time to prepare for the early lecture, in the evenings I would sit back and relax and enjoy the warmth of the bus as it was autumn by then and the evenings were chilly.

Not so one particular evening. The bus was just leaving the campus when Dermot jumped on and sat down beside me. I began to cringe as I knew he would surely act the maggot. He immediately began speaking in a very loud, Kerry accent as he pretended to be my cousin and proceeded to ask me very personal questions in a loud culchie accent.

'*There ye are now! So ye had the babby then. God yer lookin' grand but shur they say that it's the pregnancy that does it—it's de hormones. Did ye ever see a pregnant heifer? Be Jaysus the udders on her—really get ye goin'.*'

I could feel everyone on the bus staring and gobbling up every word.

'*Ah shur it's all over de place, they're all at it like feckin' rabbits up here in Dublin—the city of sin whath. Ye should have stayed in Ballygoarseup—no one to get ye up the duff there, shur they're all drunk after six. Did ye ever figure out who it was anyways—which of the three boyos?'*

I decided it was better to get off and walked away feeling every single eye boring into my back. And there he was shouting at me from the back of the bus. He would be terribly pleased with himself as he had the attention of all the passengers. Dermot was always playing to an audience. Everyone was laughing because, as well as the ridiculous things he said, he had perfected the wild-eyed, mad look of certain country caricatures.

'Mind yerself now, we wouldn't want ye havin' another accident. Remember to keep an aspirin between yer knees, that should do the trick whath. Anyways shur isn't yer poor mammy on her knees in the church sayin' novenas for ye?'

*

As the autumn moved into winter and I had known him for about four months, Dermot finally managed to convince me to take part in a crowd scene. Although I was still resisting his romantic advances, or what passed for such in his mind, I had definitely fallen for his mad sense of humour. No one before or since has ever made me laugh so much. Spending time with him was like living in the middle of a whirlwind, every day he would be a different character, and although I was often the victim of his jokes, when he wasn't around, life seemed very dull indeed. I continued to tell myself that I felt nothing for him but deep down I was falling hard. Looking back, I think I was afraid of entrusting my heart to such an unpredictable man. He could be so gentle at times, telling me about his dreams, making me feel special but then, just as quickly, he would be off on another madcap scheme—trying to break into the English department to steal the exam papers or some other whacky idea. He never actually did break in but he certainly had a love/hate relationship with the head of the English department. He always referred to his test results in tennis terms: Professor 30, Morgan 15, or, after he had written an essay that he was particularly proud of: game to Morgan! There was no doubt that I was falling under his spell but I fought hard against it.

Chapter 6

The Big Gom Cast

I still remember the evening I met the other actors. There were six or seven of them and it immediately became clear that there would be no crowd scenes. This was the beginning of one of the strangest and most intense periods of my life.

We met every day to rehearse, generally in the Italian Seminar room as there were so few people studying Italian it was almost always empty. We ate in the campus canteen every evening, usually shepherd's pie or beans on toast. We never spent much on food as we wanted to have money for beer afterwards. Dermot loved pizza and sometimes we treated ourselves but we stayed on campus where everything was subsidized, even the beer. I always drank a couple of glasses of Smithwick's while Dermot drank Guinness. We were always together, all enthralled by Dermot, we went along with everything he said. We were almost like a cult and Dermot was the undisputed cult leader. We laughed till we cried but we worked really hard too. Dermot changed his mind every day—the sketch we had been working on the previous day was thrown out the next for a new idea. If the sketch of the day was an Italian mafia one, then we kept it up in the canteen and afterwards in the bar, with Dermot doing a perfect Marlon Brando as 'The Godfather' impersonation. If the sketch was a political one, we would play the parts of ministers all day, creating hilarious schemes to make money and rip off the voters. Dermot's humour was always highly satirical, no one in the public eye got off easily and everyone was fair game to him.

I was absolutely captivated by him. He could imitate anyone, any accent, he was a constant stream of hilarious ideas. The problem was that none of us had any say as to what material was used or what was discarded. We were all under his spell. I remember Paddy, Marian,

Deidre, Barry, Brendan and Pat – all fellow students, none of us with any drama experience at all and so completely unaware of how to prepare a theatre show. Dermot's younger brother Paul, although still at high school, was usually with us. He had an even more wicked sense of humour than Dermot but was a quiet type who always shied away from the limelight and absolutely refused to take part in any of the sketches. He looked a little like Dermot but was more handsome in the classical sense. The two brothers were very close as they were to their sister, Denise. Paul never did anything with his comic talent but chose an entirely different career path. A great loss, in my opinion, as he was a wonderful mimic too. An interesting thing about Dermot's family was that they all shared a wonderful talent for caustic humour. Their sister, Denise, was no exception. They would tear strips off each other. It was never boring being with the Morgans but you sometimes felt the need for an asbestos suit! Dermot told me that they got this talent from their mother.

The fact that none of us students and cast members had any say in what material was used was a big problem as we were all living in a private world where we were in on the jokes. There was no director to remind us that the public would not get the joke, that we needed to rehearse the same sketch until it was word-perfect and could be enjoyed by outsiders too. Dermot had a brilliant comic talent but he was no director and certainly not of himself. The rest of us had no experience at all and played follow-the-leader blindfolded.

Chapter 7

The Priest's Walk

Soon after meeting him, he took me to visit the lovely, Georgian Parochial house where his mother worked. It was very grand with a long, tree-lined avenue leading up to it. It was empty the day I visited, he assured me, as I was nervous of turning up unannounced. He went inside for a few minutes as I waited on a garden seat outside, admiring the rosebushes and orderly flowerbeds. When he reappeared, I did a double take as he was wearing a long, black priest's tunic. I was aghast as I thought he had taken it from the priest's room, and I really wouldn't have put it past him but he assured me that this was not the case, it was his own. As it turned out, he had quite a selection of clerical attire made especially for him by his friend Sally. He even had a full, bishop's costume but to my great relief, he never wore it in my presence. That day at the Parochial House, he spent his time practicing the priest walk, which was head bent slightly forward and hands clasped behind his back. It was difficult for me to walk beside him as my platform heels slipped slightly on the gravel and I had to grab onto his arm for balance. Not very priestly at all but he was so funny in his imitation of the solemn tone and spiritual advice that generally veered very much off course as he talked. It went something like this.
'Tell me, my child, what troubles you? You can bare your heart to me as I never judge human weaknesses.'
'I don't know, Father, but I am indeed very troubled.'
'Tell me your thoughts, fear not as I shall not judge you.'
I would try not to laugh but it was practically impossible. His tone was so earnest as he bent his head down to hear me. I went along with the charade as best I could. I knew that he planned to put a priest sketch in the show and I wanted to please him but I didn't have

a talent for amusing dialogue. However, I tried to put myself into the part, the quiet avenue and grand house helped as they were real.

'I've been having impure thoughts', I dared to say.

'Ah, my child, a young woman is prone to many distractions. You must not allow yourself be led astray'.

'I know, Father, but there is a young man who distracts me'.

'This is very worrying, my child, as young men are often driven by a wildness in their blood, especially if they have consumed the devil's brew', he said.

'Yes, I'm afraid this particular young man is very fond of the black stuff, if you know what I mean', I answered.

'You must help him to avoid it at all costs by offering him some minerals or tea. A Baby Sham is a good alternative', he said.

At this I spluttered, as the idea of any of the group ordering a Baby Sham (watered down Prosecco for *aul* wans) was ridiculous. We always bought it at Christmas, in a six pack, for my dad's aunt who was in her late eighties. She only ever had one as she said it made her dizzy. The other five bottles always got thrown out after the holiday as absolutely no one else would drink the stuff.

'What amuses you so?', he asked, still in the part. 'I have been known to imbibe a Baby Sham myself on special occasions.'

'Nothing, Father, I will try to do as you advise', I answered solemnly.

'And with regard to your impure thoughts, you must learn to think of your body as a temple which is locked with a key. And you must keep that key close to your heart, attached to a rosary bead that you wear between your....'

Here he would stop and pretend to be in great embarrassment as he looked for a word that was not unseemly.

Giggling uncontrollably, I would make some suggestions.

'Between my breasts, Father, or between my knees?' I would ask innocently.

At this point he would start to bluster and fluster, his face growing red and his lips trembling.

'No, no', he would stammer. 'I believe it grows chilly. Let's go inside and have some apple tumble, I mean crumble. Or some tea and crumpet, I mean tea and strumpet, no, no I mean....'

By this stage I would be falling off my heels from laughing.

'There's some good stuff there that I think we can work on. We'll go over it again tomorrow with the others and see what comes out. I want the priest to be completely clueless and unable to talk to women, maybe he's even afraid of them', Dermot said.

At the time that meant nothing to me but looking back, I can see the outline of Father Dougal there, the character from the TV series, 'Father Ted'. With all the fascination he had for priests, it came as no surprise to me when he had his first television success as Father Trendy years later. And then, of course, when he became Father Ted. To my mind, it was as if he had been practicing for that role all his life and I firmly believe no one could have done it better as it was a part of him.

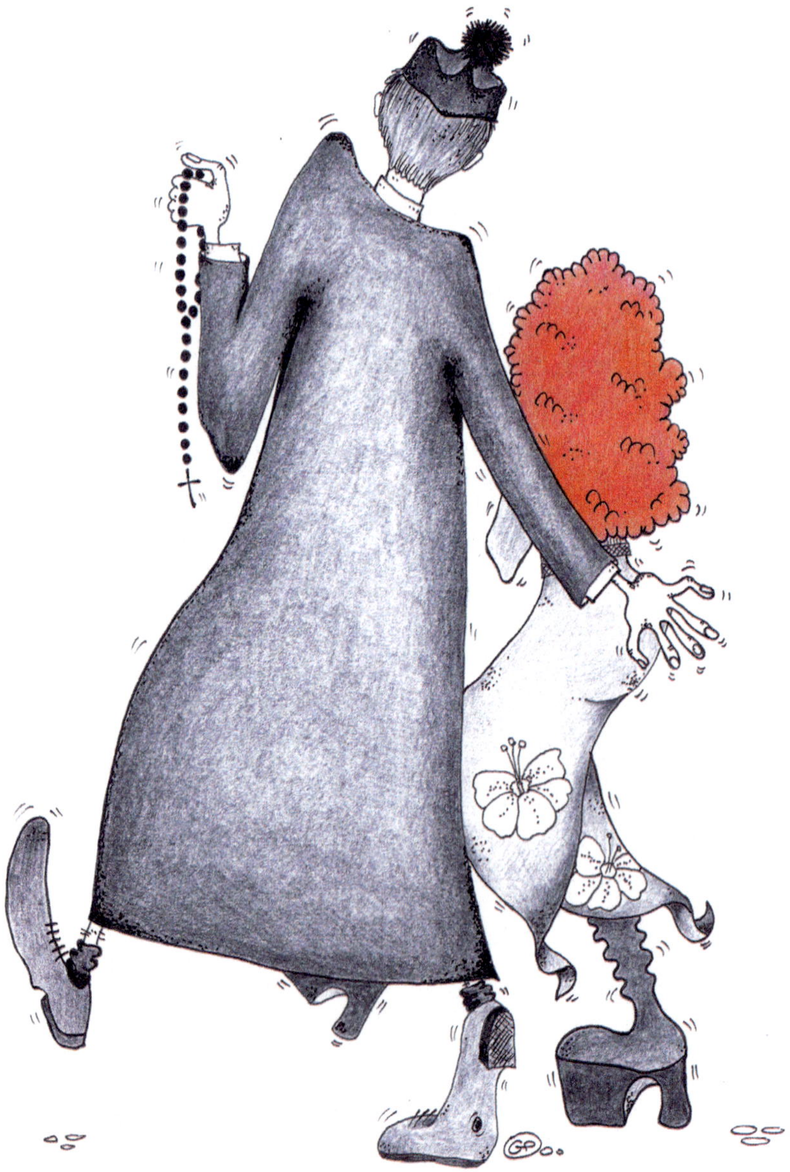

Chapter 8

A Fling

During the time that Dermot was pursuing me, I had a bit of a fling with a handsome, German professor who was spending a couple of years at UCD while he was writing a book on James Joyce. The German department was just down the corridor from the Italian one so it came about that we passed each other a couple of times a day and gave each other the once over. I have always liked big, broad-shouldered men and Gerhart was something of a Viking to look at. He had longish, blond hair and a red beard. The only thing that was missing was a helmet with horns and a sword. He was thirty-eight, which made him twenty years older than me and irresistibly attractive to a girl just out of school. There was also the fact that he behaved normally, which was a great change from Dermot's off-the-wall attentions.

Lots of girls had noticed Gerhart and there was always a rustling sound every time he appeared in the bar or canteen. This rustling sound was made by the girls, all fixing their skirts and smoothing their hair as he walked past, a little like a sudden breeze rustling through a field of wheat.

He was extremely confident and totally different to the young Irishmen of the time who never approached a girl until they were two sheets to the wind with beer. He stopped me in the corridor one day and introduced himself. He said I had a very pretty smile and would I like to have a drink with him that evening. He was so smooth you could slide off him. With my head spinning and blushing scarlet – alas, there was nothing smooth about me – I babbled something about being happy to meet him. I skipped all the way down the corridor with happiness as soon as he was out of sight. He was attracted to my curves and curls in that order, he would tell me later. We went out together for a few months. Dermot didn't know anything about this as he was often missing for days at a time and Gerhart certainly didn't want to broadcast the fact that he was going out with a student even though technically he was never a professor of mine. He knew it would have been frowned upon. My only concern was that my mother would find out as I have always belonged to that populous brigade of Irish people who proudly proclaim:

'I don't care what the world knows about me, as long as me Ma doesn't find out.'

Gerhart took me to restaurants and night clubs. I tasted Indian food with him for the first time – I can still remember the explosion of flavour in my mouth at the first forkful. I was forever hooked. It's easy to understand. I had only ever been to England where the food was as bland as it was at home and the only culinary experience I had was the Ma's cooking which consisted of burning everything to a crisp and the college canteen which wasn't much better. Gerhart had a very nice basement flat in Donnybrook, an affluent area about ten minutes from the campus, and this was where we spent most of our time. We drank white wine and listened to his impressive collection of LPs. We shared the same musical taste and he had all the records that I couldn't afford to buy. Bob Dylan, Linda Ronstadt, James Taylor, Carol King and many more. It made a nice change from going to a record shop and waiting in line to hear your favourite song. With Gerhart I had my first taste of the good life. He treated me well and was kind and generous. I was extremely flattered by his attention and he made me feel less like the awkward schoolgirl that I still was. He was also an experienced lover and gave me some much- needed confidence in my body. Before him, during my few sexual encounters, I had always been terribly embarrassed about my large breasts and would refuse to get undressed in front of my boyfriends. I literally used to get into bed in my underwear and with the light rigorously off, only then would I remove my bra and panties. When I needed to go to the loo, I would wrap the sheet around myself and scuttle to the bathroom. Gerhart wasn't having any of that. He told me that I had a great body and should show it off. He also told me that one of the things that men found most attractive was a woman confident enough to stride around naked, no matter what her shape. We went away for a couple of weekends together—study retreats, I told the Ma and in a way that's what they were, just not in the subjects she imagined. We went to Youghal, a lovely fishing village in Co. Cork and to Galway city, which is a great place for fun and music and the craic. When we stayed in hotels, Gerhart would insist that we ate our meals in the room naked. I would sit at the table or on the bed in my birthday suit trying to exude confidence but secretly cringing inside. However, he did teach me to stop scuttling and I noticed that in later relationships, the guys appreciated my self-confidence as I strode to the bathroom naked. Little did they know how much I longed to fold my arms over my breasts and make a dash for it.

I enjoyed my time with Gerhart but I have to say that there was something missing. He never made me laugh. He was a serious guy and took everything he did with the same seriousness. But I missed the sense of fun, of unpredictability that Dermot brought into my life, even though I was often exasperated by him. When he reappeared, I would smile inside although I was careful to keep up my aloof approach to him. On some level I had understood that it was the chase that intrigued him, he loved the challenge of finding ways to amuse me, to make me take risks that I would not normally take. I was careful to hide my growing affection for him, throwing my eyes up to heaven when he turned up again as if annoyed at being pestered by his attentions, when the truth was starting to be quite the opposite. He never asked any questions about what I had been doing in his absence and I never volunteered any information. Dermot was always completely wrapped up in himself, he could easily have had a double or even triple life for all I knew and I certainly never gave him the satisfaction of showing any interest in whatever he had been doing. At the same time, I kept my own double life to myself. It gave me great satisfaction to know that I

was often missing from the library when Dermot had come looking for me. I knew this as my library mates would tell me:
'Your mad Italian was here looking for you a few times'. They always referred to him as the mad Italian after his initial imitation of a love-struck Romeo, even after it became clear that he was as Irish as the rest of us.

Unfortunately, my double life was soon to come to an abrupt end. Gerhart, for all his sophistication, was no match for the Ma. When he left me home, I always made him drop me just around the corner from the house as I knew the Ma would be watching from the upstairs window—she always did when I was on the last bus home, or so she thought. But Gerhart was not wise to the ways of the Irish mammy and soon came a cropper. He had the gumption to turn up at our house unannounced one Sunday morning to take me out to lunch as a surprise. Well, I'm afraid the surprise was on him. Luck would have it that he met the Ma at the front gate as she was coming back from Mass.

He politely introduced himself and asked if he could speak to Livvy.

'And who might you be when you're up and dressed?' she asked him. He mistakenly thought that he could impress her by giving her his academic title of Professor Gerhart Hirschfield from UCD. Quick as a light, the Ma asked him:

'And since when do professors make house calls?' she quipped. By this stage they had both arrived at the front door from where I was watching the exchange, horrified.

'Just how old are you?' asked the Ma then, glaring at him. Really confused now he answered:

'I'm thirty-eight'.

'Thirty-eight are ye?! And what does a man of your age want with a young wan of eighteen? Nothing respectable, that's for sure.'

I wanted the ground to open up and swallow me but I made a belated attempt to stand up for himself.

'Mam, he's a friend of mine, let him come in and have a cup of tea.'

'I'll give him a cup of tea', she said, turning on him and brandishing her umbrella.

'Get your German arse out of here or I'll ring the university. I know all about the rules against fraternizin' with students.'

'Mam', I said, shocked, 'you can't speak to him like that.'

'I can speak any way I like in my own house. You get upstairs, I'll deal with you later. Tell your father to come out.'

At these words, Gerhart beat a hasty retreat, probably imagining some wild-eyed, war veteran with a shotgun. There was nothing I could do but burn with embarrassment as I heard his car drive away. Needless to say, my affair with the professor came to a sudden halt. I didn't doubt for a second that the Ma would really have gotten in touch with UCD if it had continued. She kept her beady eye on me for some time after that so it just wasn't worth the risk. By this I don't mean that I didn't have any feelings for Gerhart but I was not in love. I met him for a coffee about a month later and he was understandably cold and distant. How could I explain how differently sexual relationships were considered in Holy Catholic Ireland in the seventies compared to the sexual freedom that had swept through England and the continent in the sixties? It had been well and truly blocked by the Catholic Church which still ruled the country with an iron fist and I was living under the roof of one of its most stalwart champions. I had never spoken to him about the difficulties of acquiring any type of birth control for unmarried women or the amount of lies I was obliged to tell my mother just to go out with him. We parted ways with a cool kiss on the cheek and a bland 'best wishes' for the future.

Chapter 9

Contraceptives

It's time now to bring up the sticky subject of sex and contraception in Ireland in the seventies. Sex before marriage was definitely frowned upon and the age old 'I'll be careful' was about as reliable as the number 17 bus. This bus, in theory, went from the college campus all the way to Blackrock but it never actually materialized. There was a joke that went around at the time that if you wanted to commit suicide all you had to do was to lie down on the 17-bus route and you would die of hunger. All we young women could do was attend the Family Planning clinics which were illegal and constantly being shut down by our priest state. The Catholic Church ruled supreme. We had no choice but go to these clinics and sit in waiting rooms where we were looked on with disapproval by mothers of five, desperately trying not to become mothers of six. When we finally got in to see the doctor, we were given a dreadful contraption called the diaphragm which was a saucer-shaped, plastic yoke that had to be filled with a contraceptive gel and then inserted into your Dawson's Creek at some stage before you did the deed. Now you can imagine what a passion killer that was. At eighteen, the idea of finding myself 'up the duff' and even worse, having to tell the Ma, filled me with such holy terror that I found myself one evening in the bathroom of an elegant, Dublin hotel filling my cap with gel. The hotel was a posh one and the bathroom was very plush but small. I could hear women's voices outside as they went on and on in their posh accents about their day at the races. I had filled the cap with the gel which made the blinking thing very slippery and I had assumed the insert position. I don't know exactly what happened, maybe I squeezed it too hard but it flew out of my hand and propelled by the slippery gel continued on its way and scooted out under the door.

Suddenly the women stopped talking, the silence was deafening. Then the snickering started. I had no choice but to open the door, step outside and pick up the damned thing. I didn't dare go back into the toilet, I shoved the cap into some paper towels and washed my hands and left the bathroom. Maybe that was the point—the dreadful thing would put you off *shiftin'* for the rest of your life.

Chapter 10

A Perfect Day

One day Dermot was in a calm mood—practically the first time since I'd met him. We were sitting on the grass outside the library and I had taken off my jacket. I could feel the warm sun on my arms and shoulders and I knew that Dermot's eyes were on me even without looking up. He was in his usual denim shirt, he never seemed to feel the cold. We should have joined the others for a rehearsal but there was something languid in that warm air, unusual for early spring. It held the promise of something, I could feel my blood stirring. Suddenly Dermot stood up and said:

'Let's give the rehearsal a skip and go for a walk instead.'

No funny voice, no funny accent. I was intrigued. He actually talked to me as himself, I wasn't used to hearing his real voice, he was always playing some character or other. We headed out of the campus and down the long avenue that led to the main road. I had never noticed before how beautiful it was with the tall trees and branches filled with new, green leaves. He started to talk about himself. He told me about how he had lost his father at a young age and how hard it had been for his family. Because of this they were very close, he said. He talked about his mother, how they were very alike and the terrible fights they had. She had once thrown a full teapot of hot tea at him, narrowly missing his head.

'There's still the mark on the kitchen door, you will see', he said. I was moved by this new side of him. We walked and walked and he talked and talked. No jokes, no mad ideas. Just Dermot. At a certain point, he stopped and looked at me. I held my breath, I thought he was going to kiss me but instead, he caressed me gently on the cheek. He was silent for so long that I began to feel uncomfortable. Then, out of the blue, he said 'I love you.' Nothing else. He resumed walking but this time he took my hand and held it tightly in his. What was a girl to do? I had never met anyone like him. I caved. I fell. I gave in.

We went to his house. He cooked something. I thought my heart was going to explode with happiness. I had never felt anything like that before.

As we go through life certain moments remain crystal clear in our memories. Nearly forty years later I have this almost physical memory of him standing at the stove stirring something. It was peaceful in the kitchen. I remember the afternoon light coming in through the window and the strangeness of Dermot's silence. Then I experienced a wave of emotion. It was the slow realization that I actually loved this crazy, wonderful, impossible man. I went to him and put my arms around his waist and leaned my head against his back. Time stood still. He didn't turn round. I think he was shocked. It was the first time we touched.

Of course, things changed afterwards. Dermot was not an easy boyfriend. Once he had me, he didn't really know what to do with me. I couldn't cope with his mood swings. He was either euphoric or depressed. After the initial passionate phase, he went back to being his crazy self. I would have liked more alone time with him, more quiet times where he wasn't playing a part. We went out together but he often used these occasions to create some kind of scene and that made me feel that I wasn't enough for him. He seemed to always need an audience. I would live for the end of rehearsals so that I could have him to myself but even then, it was no guarantee that I could hold on to him.

Chapter 11

Lying to the Ma

When I first started going out with Dermot I was still living at home. In order to have some sort of a normal student life, it was necessary to live a double life something akin to East Germany before the unification. A big part of this consisted in telling fibs to the Ma – no easy feat as she was a walking lie detector. Out of necessity, I became good at keeping what I was up to a secret from her. I'm pretty sure I would have passed any lie detector test that the CIA or KGB could have thrown at me. Rather like a spy, I had my bag of tricks. Some very useful ones were supplied by my friend Marian who was very good on the old sewing machine. She had sewn a border of Velcro around the bottom of my very short skirts and dresses which came in handy when I ditched my long, hippy skirts in favour of a sexier look. I generally moved between the miniskirts of the sixties and hippy clothes of the seventies depending on my mood or the occasion. I was a true flower child at heart but I was well aware of the attraction the miniskirts had for men and so I took advantage of this when I went to discos or clubs. Clearly, neither style would have met with the Ma's approval. If she had had her way, I would have worn only knee-length dresses and matching coats which passed for fashion when I was making my Confirmation circa 1966. A pill-box hat in the same material was usually added and the colours were almost always pale pink, light blue or pea green. Needless to say, I would rather have been found dead in a ditch than in any of these getups but circumventing the Ma's ideas of what was respectable was no easy matter. Without Marian's help, I would never have gotten out of the house at all. On her trusted sewing machine, she had made pieces of material that I could attach to my skirts and dresses and hey presto, I passed the Ma's beady-eyed inspection as I went out the door. These extra bits were not simply plain pieces of material. Marian made them with a flounce so that when I velcroid them to the skirt or dress, they really looked as if they had been made in that style. All I had to do was once I had turned the corner, rip away the extra piece and shove it in my bag and I was ready for anything. Mary Quant would have been proud of me. My father, on the other hand, hardly ever noticed anything. I remember on one occasion meeting him unexpectedly in the street wearing a skirt that just about covered my arse and his only comment was:

'Nice belt but you'll be cold without the rest!' He never said a word to my mother and I got away with it.

Another trick I picked up for myself. Being a curvy girl, I somehow managed to look provocative in the simplest of tops so the Ma insisted that I wear nun-like high necklines that would have made even Dolly Parton look like an Amish wife. My way round this was to cut up a pair of black, silk panties and use the back part as an improvised filler-inner. The result was remarkably good and all I had to do was whip it away as soon as I was out of sight of the house and stuff it in my bag along with the fake hemline. Unfortunately, as the extra piece was not held in place with Velcro, accidents could and did happen. There was a day when I had an interview for a part-time job in a local kiddies' playgroup, run by the Sisters of the Presentation Convent, and afterwards I was meeting a handsome, long-haired guy for a drink. No problem, I thought. I wore a very low-necked, black sweater and short, black skirt. I knew the black would impress the nuns and tied my hair up in a messy chignon, no other way to do it with curls. Outside the schoolground I attached the extra length to my skirt and inserted the black silk piece into the V-neck of my sweater. I had a quick look in the bathroom mirror before going into the office for the interview and was pleased to see that I looked exactly like a novice in a convent. The interview was going very well and I was speaking animatedly about my ideas for children's games when, gesticulating, I inadvertently tore away the black piece of cloth and the Mother Superior got an eyeful of boobs as they seemed to pop out of nowhere. I desperately tried to replace the cloth and recover my modesty but alas the damage was done and I didn't get the job. This was their loss as I have always been good with children and have had a very successful teaching career but it didn't begin that day.

Dermot adored these tricks of mine and delighted in removing the extra pieces of clothing when he knew there would be maximum effect. We once attended a seminar on 'Beowulf' held by the Old English department and he specifically requested that I wear my nun's get-up as he called it. He had told me that he knew the professor well and that the lesson would be interesting but that the professor was old school and would not have appreciated my more fashionable attire. In my innocence, I believed him and wore my black sweater and skirt with the extra pieces well inserted. The seminar was long and boring and I really would have preferred to slip out but Dermot insisted on staying to the end. When it was finally over, he dragged me along to the wine and cheese reception that the department had organised. I should have known that he was up to something as these receptions were worse than having a root canal. They consisted of groups of students standing around a professor making small talk and pretending to be interested. They always served small pieces of apple and cheddar on a toothpick and plastic cups of the cheapest Valpolicella wine that could be bought from the local supermarket. Only first year students ever attended as they were hoping to make a good impression on the professors. Dermot and I joined the group that was listening to the ancient, old guy going on about Anglo-Saxon literature. The professor recognised Dermot immediately and said in a slightly ironic tone:

'Ah, Morgan, I wouldn't have expected to see you here. I don't believe you have carried out many of the assignments I set for you.'

'I'm sorry about that, professor, I know I'm a bit behind with my study schedule', answered Dermot, respectfully.

'I know all about your drama activities, it may surprise you to know that you have many admirers in the department. They tell me that they are very good fun, who knows, I may even attend the next one myself', continued the professor.

'That would be an honour, sir', answered Dermot, 'but to be truthful, I'm here this evening to accompany a young friend of mine.'

At this point, he signalled to me to come forward.

'Meet one of your new students, she is particularly interested in the Anglo-Saxon period—Olivia Connolly. She will be taking part in my next show, too. She's very talented.'

I smiled and extended my hand to shake his. Dermot moved fast and inserted himself momentarily between myself and the professor. I saw the professor's eyes practically leaping out of their sockets and, looking down, I saw that my boobs were on glorious display and I saw also that a corner of black silk was peeping out of Dermot's pocket. The poor, old guy slopped wine out of his glass and couldn't seem to be able to remove his eyes from my cleavage. Still grasping my hand, he appeared to be transfixed. There were lots of chuckles from all around as I managed to extricate my hand and move away.

'I'll bloody kill you', I hissed at Dermot as we were leaving.

'Aw come on; it was hilarious. You just made the old guy's day' was his only answer.

'I'll buy the drinks tonight to make it up to you', he added, laughing all the way to the bar.

I had other tricks too. I never gave the Ma the real phone numbers of the various friends I told her I was staying with when I didn't intend to come home so she could call as many times as she liked but all she got were wrong numbers or no answers. I did give her the numbers of a couple of friends who could be counted upon to back up any story that I had told her. We took this stuff seriously; we went through police interrogation style exercises. Let her speak, give nothing away, see how much she knows first. And of course, I had my great fall back upon stories: the bus broke down (the buses were always breaking down), the last bus was cancelled (this actually never happened but the Ma had never caught the last bus in her life so she took this at face value). I believe she even wrote an angry letter to CIE (Córas Iompair Éireann), the Irish transport company, to complain about it but they never answered. I'm pretty sure they were inundated with complaints so I didn't think I had much to worry about on that score.

Chapter 12

Phone Messages

While we were still in the early days of our relationship, I was living in Swords on the northside while he was living in the family home in Mt. Merrion on the southside. It is one of life's little coincidences but I had spent a lot of my childhood and early youth in Mt. Merrion, staying with my Mam's sister Aunt Peggy. We must have been as close as a five-minute walk for many years. I wonder if I ever bumped into him at the local shop or in the street.

In those days of no cell phones, all calls were made to the home landline over which my mother had absolute control. Having three brothers, the calls were frequent and a notepad and pen were kept beside the phone to write down messages. My youngest brother, Michael, had always great success with the ladies so on any given day there would be a list of girls' names who had called for him. He was always out and as a result, most of the messages were for him. A typical day would have gone something like this:

10.00 Louise called for M

10.25 A certain Caroline would like M to call her back

11.05 Mary-Ann is annoyed that M hasn't been in touch

12.00 Marian for Livvy – she can meet you this evening at 7.30 in the Stag's Head

12.45 Louise called again for M

13.05 Rory called for Gerry, he'll see him in the bar in Booterstown at 18.00

17.00 Mary-Ann was crying. Michael Call her!

All very boring stuff till Dermot came along. From then on, the messages became more interesting.

18.10 Elvis called for Livvy, he will meet her this evening in Neary's at 19.30

19.00 A certain David Bowie called for Livvy to say that he can't meet her this evening.

19.30 Mick Jagger for Livvy – he can meet her after all as David Bowie stood him up.

The Ma wrote all these messages down as if they were normal—granted, apart from Elvis, she probably didn't recognise any of the other names. It was only when Dermot said that Father Pearce would meet Livvy in the bar in the Shelbourne Hotel that she got upset.

'Who is Father Pearce and why are you meeting him? I'll ring the bishop if I have to, mark my words. Lord blessus and savvus, to think that any daughter of mine could be up to no good with a priest...I'll have to do the stations of the cross for ye', she would say, wringing her hands and rooting out her rosary beads.

'Calm down Ma', I would say, 'it's only Dermot messin' with ye.'

'I'll give him somethin' to mess about if I get my hands on him, the cheeky git.'

As you can imagine, I made sure that the Ma rarely came within easy distance of Dermot but I really needn't have worried. The few times that he picked me up from home he was a model of good behaviour, making polite small talk to the Ma as he drank tea in the kitchen. He could be so amenable when he wanted to, he could charm the hind legs off a donkey. The Ma would forget all about the cheeky messages and say to me afterwards:

'Now, there's a very well-mannered, young man, he's a credit to his mother.'

 He had her eating out of his hand which was one of his many talents. Little did she know that as soon as we were in his car, he'd be telling me that we were off to crash someone's party.

Chapter 13

The Loony on the Bus

An important part of every Dubliner's life has always been the amount of time spent travelling on buses. Back in the seventies these were open-backed with a steel bar to hold onto as you waited to get off. There was a space at the back where the conductor stood when he wasn't collecting the fares and it was his job to keep rowdy or drunken passengers from getting on. The sense of wit and quick repartee of the conductors was legendary as I had occasion to witness many times. Once, I got on soaking wet, and the conductor quipped:
'Drip to the front of the bus, please.' Another time I got on and the bus was literally filled with Chinese people. When the conductor came to collect my fare, he bent down and whispered to me:
'Jaysus, am I glad that you got on. I thought I was in Peking!'
In later years, the conductors were eliminated and replaced by machines and it was never the same afterwards. The drivers had no time for banter and the machines did not come with the Dublin sense of humour. But back in my heyday, travelling on the buses was fun as you had a real person to relate to. However, the most important part of the fun and games on the buses was made up of the mad characters who travelled around the city all day, constantly getting on and off as if it were their job to entertain the passengers. One of the most famous of these was undoubtedly a character called Bang Bang, whom I had the pleasure of travelling with many times as the number ten bus passed through the city centre which was his favoured stomping ground. He used to amuse us all by pointing his index finger and pretending to shoot us as he said 'bang bang!' Every now and then, some wit would play the game and fall off his seat clutching his chest, much to Bang Bang's delight.

That said, it has always mystified me the sheer number of loonies who were present on the buses back in the day. These were generally men and you could spot them a mile off and decide whether or not to travel on the bus with them or wait for the next one. The problem arose when you were already on the bus. This is how it went: you were sitting upstairs on the bus, gazing at the people waiting to get on and grateful for your window seat, when you heard a commotion downstairs. Loud voices, fractured phrases and you realised a loony had got on. You held your breath hoping that he stayed downstairs but with a heavy heart you listened to the stomping on the stairs accompanied by harsh breathing and you realised that he was coming up. You could feel the tension in the air as you waited with baited breath until he sat down. For some unknown reason, it was very often beside me. At that point, you could hear everyone else heave a sigh of relief as they relaxed and sat back to enjoy the show. Having found myself in this situation numerous times, I had come to the conclusion that it was my curly hair that attracted them. The way it floated above my head in a totally undisciplined way must have seemed like a siren call to them. During my time at university the film 'One Flew over the Cuckoo's Nest' came out and it was in that period that I was most often on the number ten bus. One evening I was sitting, minding my own business, when I heard the familiar sounds coming from downstairs. The conductor was vainly trying to prevent the loony from getting on but to no avail and sure enough, after some minutes, up the stairs he came. No! I thought, please, not me again, but sure enough, he fell into the seat beside me. I pressed myself as close to the window as I could but it did no good whatsoever as he pushed up harder against me. I kept my head stuck in my book in the hope of blocking all communication but nothing doing.

'Do you think mad people are like that?' he asked. A great opening line which dispersed my last wisp of hope that he might be normal. I ignored the question and kept my eyes firmly glued to the page as I silently cursed the people tittering around me. If there's one thing a loony thrives on, it's an audience.

'Do you now?' he repeated, prodding me in the arm. 'Do you think mad people behave like that?'

There was nothing for it but to answer.

'I'm just reading my book', I said, waving the book in the air in proof. Quick as a light, he grabbed it out of my hand and held it aloft.

'Are there any mad people in this book?' he asked. As a matter of fact, the book was 'Catch 22' and there is no shortage of mad people in it.

'Well, it depends on your definition of mad', I answered.

'So, do you know?' he asked me, then.

'Know what?' I answered, genuinely puzzled.

'Who was it? Who flew over the cuckoo's nest?' he asked.

Loud laughter from the bus—feck them all. The loony stood up; he was really getting into his stride.

'I bet you know', he said, 'with your mad hair and your books.'

Now, he was having a bit of a bad hair day himself, if the truth be told. Unexpectedly, one of the passengers took pity on me and tried to come to my rescue.

'Listen man, would you ever sit down and leave the poor girl alone', he said.

The loony did not take this well.

'I bet you know and all', was his answer. My would-be rescuer piped up again.

'Give over, you're a right bungalow', he said.

'What's that supposed to mean?', asked the loony, perplexed.

'You're a bungalow—feck all upstairs!' answered the passenger. Hoots of loud laughter greeted this comment but it did not bide well for me. I thought it best to get off.

Woody Allen has a theory. If you find yourself walking down a dark, deserted street at night, your best defence is to act strangely. Start muttering to yourself and wave your fists at the sky. Apparently, even the most hardened serial killers are nervous of mad people and will stay clear of them. I thought about that when I was on that bus but decided against it as I had no way of knowing how loonies reacted to other loonies and anyway it was a bit late for that. I decided to try another tactic. I stood up and looked my loony straight in the face. Two, fierce, blue eyes stared back at me.

I grabbed my book from his hand and shoving him out of my way, made a dash for the stairs. From there I shouted back at him:

'You're right! I do know who flew over the cuckoo's nest. It was YOU! And you have the bleedin' nest in your hair to prove it!'

And with that, I flew down the stairs amid roars of laughter from the passengers.

Dermot himself often used the buses to pull one of his stunts, always without telling me beforehand. We had said goodbye one evening at about 10 o'clock and I had left the campus on the usual number ten. He must have followed the bus by car as he got on when we were just entering the city centre. He was completely rat-arsed or so he wanted to appear. I knew for a fact that he hadn't even had one drink. In all the time I knew him, I never saw him drink a lot, and absolutely never drunk. He didn't need the prop of alcohol; he was perfectly capable of getting up to all kinds of high-jinks while being stone-cold sober. But of course, he could play the drunk to perfection. I was sitting at the back of the bus and spotted him immediately when he got on. I nearly had a canary when I saw him as I thought to myself 'here we go again'. He stayed close to my seat, swaying and falling over and generally making a nuisance of himself. I pretended not to know him from Adam. The conductor attempted to get him to pay his fare and he went into a routine worthy of Laurel and Hardy as he tried to get his hand into his pocket without falling flat on his face. He was holding onto the pole and swinging wildly every time the bus went around a corner and he would let go of the pole to try and take his money out. When he eventually succeeded, he pulled out a load of coins which of course he dropped on the floor.

'Ah Jaysus', said the bus conductor, 'another one who's been out on the batter. I've had enough. Here lads, let's get him off.' This latter was said to a couple of young fellas who were sitting near me. This was easier said than done as the 'drunk' was now on all fours, scrabbling around trying to pick up the coins. The poor passengers who were trying to get off the bus had to clamber over him but he always stood up just at the same moment, creating havoc. This was pure pantomime. The bus driver changed tactics and tried to get him to sit down but he had no intention of doing that. The whole bus was in an uproar and Dermot was in his element. He swayed around the pole, falling on top of me as he pretended to be about to puke. Some people were tut-tutting and giving him dirty looks but he wasn't a bit bothered. On the contrary, he burst into song or what passed for singing. A ridiculous version of 'Seven Drunken Nights' with the words all mixed up. I couldn't help myself, I burst out laughing and he winked at me. One woman commented:

'A very appropriate choice of song, if ye could sing it', she stated.

'Would ye look at the state of ye! God help de poor woman who's waitin' for ye to come home. I wouldn't let ye in the door', another woman said angrily.

'Ah, I'd say ye would, go on, give us a smacker, I bet it's been a long time since you had a good ride', answered the 'drunk' cheekily.

Most of the passengers were laughing and enjoying the scene. There were few things Dermot enjoyed more than getting on 'old biddies' wicks. And there was always one who would pipe up and start complaining. Fuel to his fire.

'Ah, go on with ye now, shur ye wouldn't kick me out of bed on a cold evenin'. I could show ye a good time', he answered as he moved closer to her to try and give her a drunken smacker.

'Holy Mother, is this what de country's come to? A decent, God-fearing woman can't get on a bus without being harassed by a drunken slob. It's de damn drink that's de curse of the working classes, get yer slobbering hands away from me', she answered outraged.

'*Ye've got that wrong, missus, it's de dam work that's the curse of the drinkin' classes*', Dermot answered to whistles and loud applause from the passengers. Even the bus conductor was grinning.

He then turned his attention to me.

'*Yer a grand-lookin' girell, where'd ye get dem luvvly currels?*' I ignored him but he wasn't giving up. He was in full performance mode.

'*Arr ye off to meet yer fella? He's a lucky fekker, dat's for shur. Where is he takin' ye? Ye'd have a better time with me, I can promise ye.*'

The old biddy, who should have known better, put in her spake again.

'*And where would ye take her in de state yer in?*' she asked haughtily.

'*Cloud nine, that's where I'd take her*', answered the 'drunk'.

This retort had the whole bus laughing uproariously.

'As if you'd be able to find it in your state. You're so blotto you couldn't find your own dick in your trousers.'

This was said by one of the young lads sitting next to me. I didn't like the tone of it and he had the hardened expression of someone looking for a fight. It was time to get off the bus and end the 'show'. This was often the problem with Dermot's impromptu street theatre. While Dubliners generally went along with the gag and enjoyed it, there was often an undertone of aggressiveness in young, Dublin men, especially late in the evening. No doubt, this boy had also 'had a few' and was gunning for a 'barney' as a street fight is called in Dublin slang. Dermot did not have an aggressive bone in his body and always withdrew quickly when the tone of the crowd started to change. On this occasion, when I got off the bus, he followed me but stayed in the part by falling down the steps and lying sprawled on the pavement. I waited for him around the corner.

'That was fun, wasn't it?' he asked me.

'It was', I said, 'but I'm more interested in cloud nine', I answered.

'Pray, me Lady, follow me to my carriage and I will conduct you there forthwith', he answered.

There was never a dull moment with Dermot, that I can guarantee.

Chapter 14

Going Out with Elvis

Early one evening we were 'having at it' as my mother would say if she ever talked about sex, which of course she didn't, when the phone rang. We were in his room in his family home and the phone was on the hall table. Much of our intimacy was conducted in the afternoons or early evenings as he always had so much going on. There was never a lot of time for long interludes or lazy mornings in bed. At the sound of the phone, he immediately lost interest in me.

'You're not really going to answer that NOW?', I asked him in dismay.

'It might be important', he answered, already throwing some clothes on. He went out to the hall and was back in a few minutes, breathless with excitement.

'It's Brendan Balfe', he said, 'he wants to meet up.'

He was dressed and out the door before I had time to realise what was happening. I watched from the window as I heard his old, blue Toyota roar up Wilson Road and disappear into the grey evening drizzle. Shivering, I pulled my Aran sweater over my head and felt the dull, familiar ache. I knew there was never any point hanging around waiting for him to come back. It could have been late that night or just as likely, he would not come back at all. Brendan Balfe was an important contact as he had his own show on RTÉ (Raidió Teilifís Éireann), the Irish television network. It was some consolation to me that on that particular occasion Dermot managed to convince him to come and see the show. This would have been a game changer for him as Balfe could have facilitated his entry into the magical world of RTÉ.

Occasionally, I did try to speak to Dermot about how I felt when he treated me in this way. As we were very much an unofficial couple and we both lived separate lives, it wasn't easy to pin him down. Trying to tie Dermot down was like trying to hold water in your hands. I knew better than to make demands on him, that would have had him running for the hills straight away. I had learnt that the best way to keep him in my life, and I very much wanted that, was to carry on an independent life of my own. I kept a certain air of mystery about what I was doing, which was generally spending evenings watching old movies, but I made sure he didn't know that. I sometimes went away for weekends which he didn't like, so I did it more often.

As always with Dermot, there was a funny side to this too. We both had a real thing for Elvis and had been to see the film 'That's the Way It Is' (a documentary film on the King of Rock 'n' Roll) several times. When we came out, I would spend the whole evening with the King! I have always considered Elvis's voice the sexiest ever, even when he was just speaking, and Dermot could imitate him perfectly. When I told him how I felt—neglected, lonely, used—he would listen seriously for about five minutes and then he would answer me in the rich, silky tones of Mississippi and I would hear Elvis speaking. His imitation was beyond perfect, all I had to do was close my eyes and I could imagine I had the sexiest man on earth whispering in my ear.

'Aw honey, I guess I haven't been lovin' you right. Hand on my big ole heart, I will make it up to you. You know I don' wanna lose you.'

Then he'd start crooning 'I Just Can't Help Believing' and I'd be lost. It was mesmerizing. He took role play to a whole new level. I would find myself in bed with Elvis. It was a huge turn on and for a while I would forget about my grievances.

Chapter 15

The Priest in the Pub

We were having a drink in a Dublin pub one evening when I spotted my beautiful cousin Geraldine. She was all the talk of the family at that time as she had recently started going out with a wealthy up-and-coming businessman. Sure enough, she was sitting with him at a table not far from us. Dermot and I were discussing whether or not to go to a party afterwards. Suddenly he said:

'Why don't you introduce me to your cousin?' I mistakenly thought he was being nice and I went over to her and asked them if they would like to join us. They accepted and we chatted normally for a while. To my surprise Dermot behaved impeccably. He even went as far as to invite them to come with us to the party. It was Saturday evening, they said they didn't have any plans, so we finished our drinks and went up to the bar to pay. As usual, I had Dermot's wallet and keys in my bag and when the barman came over Dermot immediately said that he would pay. I groaned inwardly as I knew what was coming next. He started to rummage in my bag while making sure that his wallet was sticking up, perfectly visible to all. He would continue to search all the while berating me on the fact that he could never find anything in my bag. We all looked at his wallet but no one said anything. Then out of embarrassment, Geraldine's boyfriend took out some money and paid the bill. I gave Dermot a dirty look but he ignored me. He always pulled this stunt with people he didn't know well. It was just a joke to him, he liked to see the expressions of people as they watched him root around pretending to look for his wallet. He was not mean at all; he just couldn't resist getting a rise out of people. He would sometimes leave me small presents in my bag- a bar of chocolate or a bag of sweets but these kind gestures were somewhat ruined when he would say to people that I was anyone's for a bag of Liquorice All Sorts. This was completely untrue; they would have had to throw in a couple of Walnut Whirls as well.

My cousin and her boyfriend were following us in their car. Having led them about half an hour out of the city, Dermot suddenly did a U-turn in the middle of the street with a screech of brakes and horns blowing madly, and turning to me he said:

'Let's lose them!' This was Dermot. I was obliged to make up some ludicrous excuse that no one believed. My mother and aunt were not impressed. My cousin didn't speak to me for ages.

I never knew what to expect from him. One evening we had arranged to meet in a pub in the city centre, Mulligans in Poolbeg Street, a favourite of ours as it had never been gentrified and still kept all the characteristics of a Dublin pub, with various snugs— separate drinking spaces with armchairs and a table where you could speak in private—, a large open bar at the back with lots of tables very close together and a roaring fire. I was always the first to arrive as Dermot was perennially late but, even so, I wasn't in time for a snug and had to make do with a small table and two stools in the middle of the large, back room. The pub was full, everyone talking in loud voices and there was a haze of smoke over everything. When Dermot arrived, people suddenly went quiet. As soon as I saw him, I understood why. He was dressed as a priest. He walked in and gave a wry smile to everyone and a type of shy salute. The people present nodded at him respectfully. He sat down and smiled at me as if there was nothing out of the ordinary. I tensed as I knew that he was up to no good. He ordered a glass of Bailey's from the barman who had suddenly appeared at our table. This was practically unheard of in Mulligan's as, generally, you had to fight your way to the bar and shout your order over the counter. He then proceeded to spend the whole evening trying to put his hand up my skirt in front of the shocked people sitting nearby. A woman of about fifty was sitting at the table nearest to us. She kept looking over and glaring at Dermot and myself. She was wearing a headscarf and still had her rain mac on even though the pub was stifling hot. She continued to look at us as she clearly complained about Dermot's behaviour to the quiet man sitting next to her. Strangely, he didn't seem to mind at all and actually tried to shut her up!

'A disgrace to the cloth,' she finally said to Dermot, obviously overcome with righteous anger.

'Sure, she's my favourite niece', said he with a lewd grin. 'I'm taking her out for a special treat. Would ye like me to say a Mass for ye?'

'You shouldn't be saying Mass', she answered, 'you should be stripped of the cloth.'

'Speaking of stripped', he said to me, 'get your bag, we're off to that new night club on Leeson Street.'

The woman almost had an apoplectic attack. She was red-faced with anger as she continued to berate Dermot, threatening to call the bishop. He stood up and gave a kind of blessing to the people around us as we left. Some of them were clearly annoyed but others were grinning—they weren't fooled.

Dermot was delighted with himself when we left, there was nothing he liked more than shocking people. He especially loved mocking the Catholic Church and priests in particular.

Chapter 16

The Coffee Dock

My scholarship covered my fees and books and I had a small amount to live on. It would probably have been enough if I had continued to live at home but I wasn't prepared to do that, and I definitely needed to get out from under the Ma's iron fist. I'd been saving up for my own place since I was seven years old and I know that for sure as I began my savings fund with my Communion money. That said I had to find a part-time job. I worked for a while in Captain America's in Grafton Street. This was one of the new American-style burger restaurants that had opened up in Dublin just a few years previously. It was on the first floor and had windows looking out on the lively, urban scene of Grafton Street. Loud American rock music blasted from the speakers and you had to speak up to be heard. There were colourful posters on the walls, pictures of famous American rock singers and bands and large photos of iconic US cities. It was a young person's place, even the kitchen staff were all university students. I remember the guy who made the pizzas had a degree in philosophy and the burger guy had a masters in economics. The seventies were tough years for anyone looking for a serious job, but they were fun times if you were footloose and fancy-free. I enjoyed working there with all those interesting guys around as lots of flirting and hanky-panky went on. But the pay wasn't enough to allow me to get a place of my own so I kept looking around for other opportunities. Soon enough, I was lucky enough to land a real game-changer of a job when I was hired to work at The Coffee Dock inside the New Jury's Hotel in Ballsbridge, on the graveyard shift. This was the only restaurant in Dublin that was open twenty-four hours a day as the sign outside proclaimed but this wasn't true. It actually closed for an hour between five and six AM. This led to countless rows with

Guinness-filled jerks who refused to accept that we were closed and usually ended up sleeping the hour away in the carpark.

If Captain America's had been the 'in' restaurant of the time, then the Coffee Dock was about as out as you could get. The hotel itself was very elegant, I'm speaking here of the Coffee Dock in particular. Captain America's attracted the 'in' crowd of young student types, the Coffee Dock attracted the dregs of Dublin society, I am referring to the night shift only as during the day it functioned as a normal coffee shop. Our customers were people who staggered in after the pubs closed at about one AM and then again at around three AM after the nightclubs shut their doors. The nightlife in Dublin city during the seventies wasn't any great shakes. The nightclubs were mainly on Leeson Street and Baggot Street and were the only places open after the pubs closed. They served over-priced wine until dawn and were generally a bit dodgy. The only way they could have a license to serve alcohol after midnight was to pretend that they were restaurants and they were often raided by the police. For this reason, they would hurriedly stick a dirty plate with some leftover food on the table in front of you minutes before the police arrived. They had names like: The Pink Elephant, Zhivago, Leggs, and Maxwell Plums.

The Coffee Dock was very much a Dublin institution and part of the after-party scene. It consisted of rows of banquette tables with seats that you had to slide into and there was a counter at each end with stools. The décor was based on the American diner but the reality was very much that of an Irish, country hotel with naff carpets and Formica-covered tables, with elevator-type music on a loop that luckily was low enough to ignore. Zilch atmosphere and overall depressing. The menus were covered in plastic and practically nailed to the tables. Dermot never actually ate there although he did sometimes give me a lift to work. The graveyard shift started at ten PM and finished at seven AM. It really wasn't Dermot's kind of place; the clientele was often drunk and disorderly and he was never inspired to pull off any of his usual skits there. It wasn't his kind of audience and it wasn't anyone's kind of food. The drunken customers were a real problem for the waitresses as the men tended to assume that we were on the menu too. These drunks were one of the reasons why the hotel found it so hard to keep staff. Very often, one or another of the girls, having been molested one time too many, simply gave up and left. But we had a champion who looked out for us. When one of us girls was having a tough time with a customer, we had our own, personal knight in shining armour in the shape of a five-foot hero of a man from Kildare called Charly. He was part of the cleaning staff and protecting the waitresses was not part of his job description but Charly had very high ideals of male chivalry and would come running at the first sign of trouble. He would pound down the hall shouting and brandishing his hoover at the guilty party. His roar was enough to put the fear of God in them and they would stagger out pursued by Charly and his hoover. We would reward him with hugs and kisses and we in our turn leapt to his defence whenever he was berated by the supervisor for leaving his post. He saved me many times and I really don't think I could have continued to work there without his gallant actions.

The work was hard as we were run off our feet. Half of the staff were middle-aged women who were working the night shift so they could look after their children during the day. Many of them were single mothers or married to unemployed men who spent their time drinking the days away. These women lived hard lives and this hardness was etched on their faces. They had very deep lines and dark circles under their eyes. They can't have gotten more than three or four hours sleep a night. Their characters reflected this same hardness, both towards the customers and towards the younger, part-time members of the staff. They kept to themselves and never intervened to help us out when we were being mauled by some drunken slob. They knew that for us this was only an interval, a chance to earn some money before we moved on to a better life. For them this WAS their life and they were quite antagonistic towards us. The other half of the staff was made up of young women who worked on a part-time basis. They were generally not students but girls who were between jobs or doing secretarial courses during the day. We bore the brunt of the slobbery attempts at seduction but stood up for each other and always intervened when a customer was out of line, with Charly's help. We stuck together and helped each other out, lending a hand when one of the girls was overrun with customers by clearing her tables and taking some of the orders. We joked and laughed and made the most of a bad situation. We all had to wear a uniform, an ugly monstrosity in the form of a shapeless, orange dress, mercifully covered by a white apron. There had been some sort of loophole in the original contract for the staff on the night shift which gave them a percentage of the takings. I have no idea how this came about but I know it created a lot of animosity with the day-shift employees. I didn't care, the Coffee Dock took in huge amounts of money so our pay was really high and by working two or three nights a week I was able to finally afford a place of my own.

Not only was the pay great but we also received huge tips. I still remember the evening I received a tip of fifty pounds from an Australian man. I was so sure he'd made a mistake that I pointed it out to him but he assured me that he was simply pleased with the service. The tips were shared and we decided to blow the fifty pounds on two bottles of champagne. Naturally, we invited Charly to join in our celebration but didn't invite any of the supervisors.

The job had other attractions too. Everyone who was anyone stayed at the hotel at one time or another and would come into the Coffee Dock. I got to see lots of famous people: the international rugby teams always stayed there, Sean Connery and Julia Roberts too, to name but a few and I'm happy to say that I met a personal favourite of mine. I had long been a Thin Lizzy fan and had seen them play live in Dublin a couple of times. I had been lucky enough to catch them at their earliest gig in a school hall in Cloughran, near Dublin Airport, in 1970 as I was going out with a boy from the school where they played. I became an immediate fan and fell head over heels in love with Phil Lynott who was the first black, Irish rock star. I loved his huge Afro hairstyle and sexy voice. I had seen them play again in Blackrock Park in Dublin in 1971. They became famous in 1973 with a rock version of the traditional Irish ballad 'Whiskey in the Jar' and went on from there to become one of Ireland's most successful rock bands ever with the songs 'Jailbreak' and 'The Boys are Back in Town'. My personal favourite is 'Parisinenne Walkways', played with another world- famous, Irish musician, Gary Moore. You can imagine my excitement then when I heard that the band was over from England and staying at the hotel. I worked an extra night's shift in the hope of seeing them but they never came in. I had almost given up hope when, on a quiet Sunday morning, I was manning the bar alone at about three AM. The other girl was on her break and the bar was empty when Phil Lynott himself appeared in the doorway. I held my breath as he walked a little unsteadily to the bar and sat down on one of the stools. He was wearing black, leather trousers and a black tee-shirt and all I could think was 'sex on legs!' He looked a little lost and he seemed to have trouble focusing. I approached him and in an awestruck voice asked him what he wanted to drink. He looked at me with the most soulful, brown eyes I had ever seen and said:

'You have luvly hair.' To which I replied, 'So have you.' This response was obviously too much for him as he slid off the stool and onto the floor with a graceful, fluid movement. I stood there dumbstruck. I had no idea what to do. Then two of his security guards came in and carried him out. It was short and sweet but I've never forgotten the night I met Phil Lynott.

There were difficulties too in the form of the Head Chef. He was a right hard ass from the inner-city with a bad attitude and even worse cooking skills. He took his anger out on us poor waitresses and we all lived in terror of him. His name was Mick and he was the scourge of my life as he had it in for me in particular as I was a college girl. To give you an idea of just how bad his cooking was, we, the staff, were entitled to a free meal per shift but all of us brought a packed lunch from home.

The menu consisted of what passed for Irish cuisine in the seventies. There was the ever present 'Full Irish breakfast' — beloved of our drunken customers as it was supposed to be great for mopping up the ten pints of Guinness, as I was informed by said customers more than once—, roast chicken and chips, beef or chicken curry, a 'risotto' that had more to do with the leftovers than any Italian dish, and chicken Maryland.

One evening two well-dressed Englishmen came in and sat down at one of my tables. There was a particular thing about the Coffee Dock, one table had a clear view of the kitchen. Chance would have it that these two men sat at that table. One of them ordered the risotto. After a few minutes he called me over and said that he wanted to change his order as he had just seen the chef pick up the rice with his hand. As we were the only restaurant open, he had no choice but to stay put.

'I'll have the chicken Maryland instead', he said. I have no idea why this dish was called chicken Maryland as all it consisted of was a chicken drumstick with a pineapple ring placed on top. Nervously, I went up to Mick and, keeping myself at a safe distance, I told him that a customer wished to change his order.

'And why is that?' he asked in a quiet voice which was even more chilling than his usual rough tones.

'He said that he saw you pick up the rice with your hands', I answered, moving myself to an even safer distance.

'Did he now?' he continued in the same icy tone. 'And what, tell me, would he like instead?'

'The chicken Maryland', I replied, expecting him to roar at me at any moment—it wouldn't have been the first time. But he stayed very still.

'Tell him', he said, 'that I pick up the pineapple ring with my mickey!'

Chapter 17

Housemates

During this period, I finally managed to move out and get my own place. It was a house in Goatstown, which was about twenty minutes from college, and I shared it with four other students. My housemates were a motley group—three guys and a girl. I had a nice big room at the front thanks to my job at the Coffee Dock and I really enjoyed this house-sharing.

When Dermot came to the house we stayed in my room. I was jealous of the personal time I had with him and never wanted to spend it with others. I already had to share him with the cast members at rehearsals. He would generally swing by on his way to or from some meeting or other. He was forever hatching some scheme and was often missing for days at a time.

As a result, I spent a lot of my time with the other housemates. One I remember particularly, as he was slightly odd and didn't fit in with the rest of us. His name was Seamus and he was from Northern Ireland. He was a lacto-vegetarian and, up until then, I had no idea they even existed. He was an absolute fanatic about what he put in his body and we were all subjected to long lectures on the evils of packaged food and the horrors of takeaways. While the rest of us survived on bacon and eggs, beans on toast and orange cheddar sandwiches with crisps, not to mention—God forbid—curries, he was always at the stove making some evil-smelling concoction that he would try in vain to get us to try.

It didn't help his cause that he was a clammy-skinned, sickly type with a permanent cold. I remember sitting in the kitchen eating a Club Milk while he berated me on the poison I was consuming.

'*De yooy know what krapp yere putting into your boddah?*' he said to me.

This was accompanied by a fit of coughing and spluttering that made me move back as far as I could from him. I sat there all rosy cheeked and glossy haired waiting for him to recover and when he did, on he would go.

'*Hawv yooy any idear wots auctually in dot biscutt?*'

More coughing and spluttering. I would calmy continue to enjoy my Club Milk.

'Way to go, Seamus!', I used to say to him, 'Keep it up, you'll soon be ready for the sanitorium!'

He never laughed. He used to put his concoctions in the fridge with little notes saying, 'Do not eat this!'—as if! Sometimes we would throw them out as they smelt so bad and he would rant at us saying:

'*Have yee nooh respect*?!' His rants were totally ineffectual as they were always interrupted by him sneezing and we would just walk off and leave him there.

The rest of us got on very well and had a nice, easy-going attitude to the food in the fridge. We were welcome to eat anything that was there as long as we replaced it. We also had a tradition of a Sunday-evening curry together. Seamus never participated but he would sometimes come into the kitchen and start to lecture us until we got fed up and chased him out waving a curried chicken leg at him. He would escape upstairs and lock himself in his room as if the devil himself was pursuing him while we merrily drank cheap wine and tucked into prawn crackers.

Chapter 18

Gate-crashing

For all the time that I knew him, Dermot was obsessed with getting into RTÉ. To this end, he did everything he could to meet people who worked there and he sometimes used me to do it. He was obsessively driven to succeed in television to the exclusion of everything else. He had a very clear vision of exactly where he wanted to go and nothing and no one was going to stand in his way. He wanted his own comedy show, where he would be writer, director and actor. He was incredibly gifted and coupled with his determination, I never doubted that he would succeed. I knew that personal relationships would always take second place to his ambition and he was not averse to using people to get what he wanted. He never hid this side of himself, the question is why we all went along with it, why I went along with it. It was partly due to his great, personal charisma. After you had spent time with him, everything else seemed incredibly dull. We all vied for his attention, gloried in it when he bestowed it on us and felt disappointed and hurt when he turned that attention elsewhere. As his 'girlfriend' I suffered more than the others, hanging around waiting for him to seek me out and being grateful when he did. In life, I am not a pushover but when it came to Dermot, I became one. I had held back my feelings for so long, had played the part of the unimpressed for so many months that the feelings I had for him had grown out of control to the extent that I could not do without him. If I had relented earlier and allowed our relationship to take its course naturally, those feelings would have surely burnt out very quickly in the cold reality of Dermot's affections. As it was, I found myself unable to break away, putting his needs before mine and desiring his success almost as much as he did.

Years later, I was still following his progress from afar. Although he was the boyfriend who treated me with the least consideration, I never felt any bitterness towards him. I wanted him to make it and when he had his first success on the radio with 'Scrap Saturday', I was delighted for him. I knew that he went through some hard years of bitter disappointment and my heart broke for him. When, much later, he finally reached the pinnacle of success with the TV show 'Father Ted', I was overjoyed for him. I felt that he had finally received the recognition he deserved and that all was right with the world.

When I said he used me to meet people who worked for RTÉ, I meant that he used my curvy figure to help him get into places from which he would be excluded. We would arrange to meet for a drink —Neary's pub just off Grafton Street was one of our favourite watering holes. It was an old-fashioned pub and it still had the stained carpet on the stairs that was coming loose on some of the steps and upstairs it had the same, old, red armchairs that had been there since its grand opening in 1889. As it was so close to the Gaiety Theatre, it had always been a favourite with actors and theatre-goers and its wrought-iron lanterns and guilt mirrors, by then more than a little tarnished, still held some of that glamour. In a way, it seemed fitting that a budding actor like Dermot should feel so much at home there. We always went upstairs to the lounge which was generally quieter than the bar downstairs, where the snugs were always full and the tables and chairs were so close together that it was impossible to have a private conversation. The walls were decorated with theatre posters and black and white photos of actors and actresses of the past. On one occasion—the fault of the infamous platform boots and the loose carpet—I actually managed to fall up the stairs. Dermot said it was some kind of record—I was probably the first person in the world to succeed in falling upstairs. He really gave me a hard time over those boots. Once we drove out to Killiney Bay and walked on the sand. I was wearing the boots and kept sinking and Dermot said it was like going out with a midget. He was such a romantic.

Sometimes, at the weekend, we would arrange to meet in Neary's and he would say to me:

'Wear something sexy.' I knew then that he was planning one of his raids. Sure enough, he would arrive into the pub like a whirlwind saying: 'Come on quick! There's a party at Gay Byrne's house. I think we can get in!'

He'd drag me up from the table and out to the car with me trailing my bag, jacket and whatever book I'd been reading. Once in the car, he'd be talking nineteen to the dozen about how he had found out about the party and what possible tactics we could use to get in. These usually involved me chatting up the security guard/doorman and flashing my boobs enough to distract them while he slipped inside.

Gay Byrne was the most famous TV personality of the time. His Saturday night talk show was one of the highlights of the week and was watched by young and old. There would be a panel of guests ranging from actors to politicians, writers to sports heroes and anyone who had come into the public eye for whatever reason. There was always a musical interlude and young musicians would sell their grannies to get a spot on the show. Gay himself was a very pleasant man by all accounts but it wasn't possible to just stop him in the street. You would need an introduction. Dermot's plan was to somehow gate-crash the party and maybe manage to have a few words with the man himself. He lived in a beautiful mansion house in Howth, a pretty, fishing village just north of the city. It only took us about fifteen minutes to get there by car. However, as soon as we neared the house that evening, we realized that there wouldn't be any possibility of sneaking in unnoticed. It was invitation only and there was a long line of cars backed up in front of the entrance. Two security men were checking invitations through the car windows, there was no chance of me flashing my boobs in the darkness and confined space of the car. Disappointed, we turned around and headed back to the city centre.

We never managed to get into Gaybo's house but we were more successful with other lesser VIPs. Once inside, things always followed the same pattern—he'd be off immediately to hook up with the important person and I'd be left all by myself trying to look inconspicuous in a room full of strangers. He would forget about me completely to the point where, on one occasion, I actually saw him dash past me in his rush to crash some, more useful event without stopping to take me with him.

These were never easy occasions for me. When I managed to get him inside, I was happy and proud of my success. I felt useful to him and this was important to me. He would be in a very good mood afterwards and would reward me with passion once we were alone. These intimate moments with him were precious to me as he was often distracted, his mind racing with some new scheme.

However, when he forgot about me and left me behind, it was no laughing matter. The bus service stopped running at 11.30 PM and the houses of the VIPs were never exactly on the main bus route. I was often lucky enough to attract the attention of some man who would give me a lift home. The difficulty was getting out of the car when we arrived there. In general, however, Irish men were gentlemen and a firm 'no' was sufficient. When this happened, I would be careful not to be seen by Dermot for a couple of days. 'Let him worry about where I am and who I'm with for a change', I would tell myself but it was a meagre consolation.

There was no point at all in being jealous or possessive where Dermot was concerned. I never knew where he was or what he was up to. Sooner or later, he would turn up and I would be dragged into his crazy world all over again. He was forever making contacts, following up on other contacts or plotting how to meet this person or that. He was tireless in his pursuit of the chance to break into television. Nothing stood in his way.

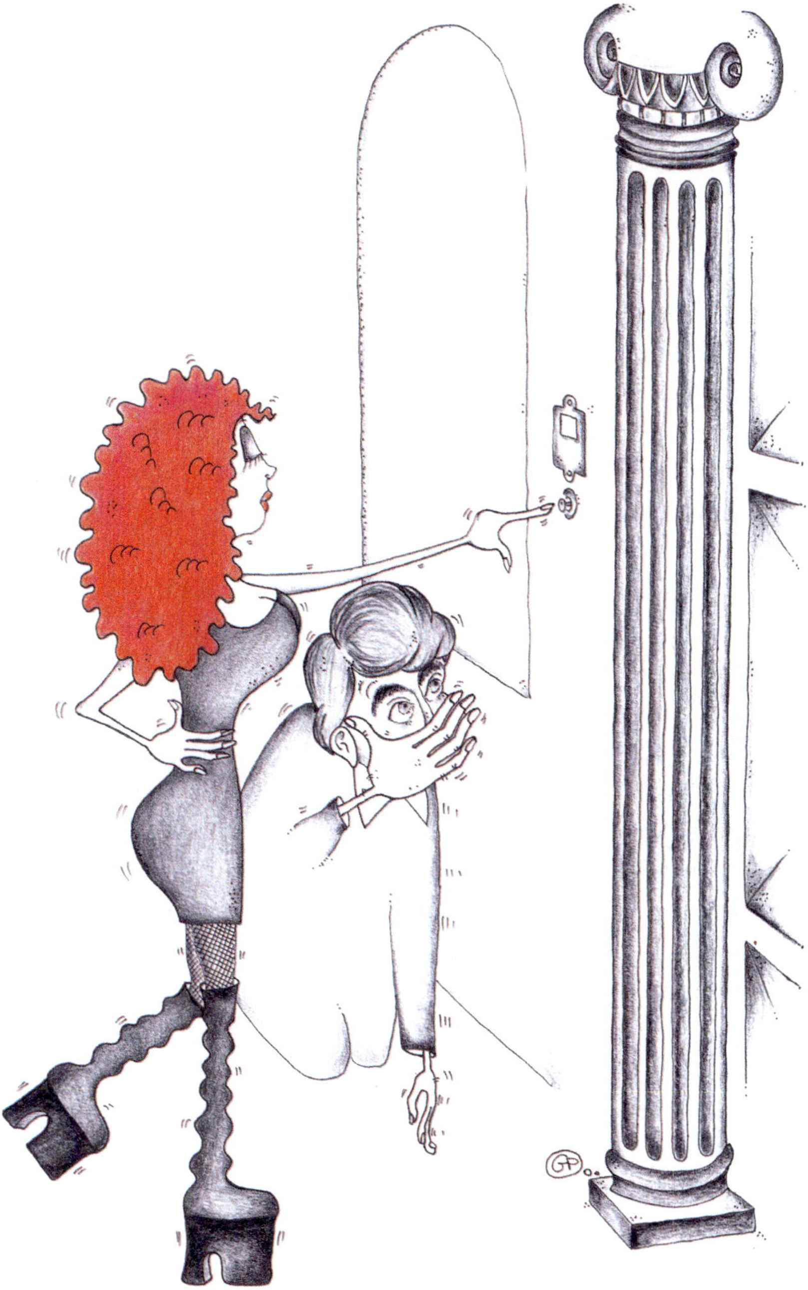

Chapter 19

The Cast Part II

When I wasn't involved in Dermot's manic world, I lived the life of a normal student, going to lectures and studying in the library. And then, of course, there were the rehearsals for the show.

Apart from Dermot himself, there were about eight of us involved, none of us with any previous experience of any kind. Dermot wrote all the sketches but as we practiced, we all made our own contributions. However, none of it mattered as Dermot always changed everything and expected us to keep up with him. The only one of us who was able to ad lib like him was his brother Paul, but he flatly refused to participate in the show. He came to all the rehearsals and his quick wit added a lot of humour to the work but he could not control Dermot any more than we could. Dermot had the last word. Each and every time.

There were a number of sketches and these made up the first half of the show. The second half was musical, a parody of country music followed by an Elvis tribute. I was part of the back-up singers. Dermot wanted to call us The Tampons but we objected and after much discussion we finally settled on The Tampettes. We each had our own sketch which we practiced diligently but it was to no avail as Dermot constantly modified everything and we simply couldn't keep up with him.

One of the most amusing members of the cast was Paddy. Dermot had a great talent for finding extremely funny people who were so utterly shy that they would never threaten his place centre stage. Paddy was one of these. A tall, lanky fellow with long hair and a guitar hung over his back, he was from Dublin city and was studying philosophy. He would often quote Sartre or Kant at the most unlikely moments. These quotes always sounded strange as he had a really strong Dublin accent.

'*We haf te remember dat it's only de person who isn't rowin' who has time to rock de boah.*'

We would all stop talking and burst out laughing. He would say:

'*What are yis laughin' at? Dat's not me dah said dah—it was Saart.*'

Or when one of us was annoyed about something he would shake his head and say:

'*Hell is oder people.*'

He produced these jewels completely out of the blue. He was a gentle soul who believed that Sartre could have done with a few pints of de black stuff. He had the Dublin gift of repartee. He was also a terrible womanizer and would often turn up at rehearsals with a different girl in tow. Strangely they never seemed to get angry with him, I don't remember any jealous scenes. It must have been the philosophy quotes. I once heard him say to one of his girlfriends who was stressing him a bit:

'*He who tinks great toughts often makes great mistakes.*'

He got away with it all because it was impossible to get angry with him. We once called round to the house he shared with an American guy. He told us that Paddy was in his room and that he would tell him we were there. He came back and said:

'He'll be down in a minute.'

We sat in the kitchen waiting for him when after a few minutes we heard an unmistakable sound coming from upstairs—a headboard knocking against a wall—and we all roared laughing. The American guy said:

'Ah, that's Paddy all right, spreadin' the love.' When we gave him a hard time over his women he would say:

'*A man can't step twice in de same river—dah's not me, dah's Heraclitus.*'

Paddy was in a few of the sketches and he played the guitar in the musical part.

Next, there was Marian. I had met her in the queue for the bookshop and we immediately struck up a friendship. Very pretty and with a smile that would have put Julia Roberts to shame, she was studying English and French. When Dermot dragged me into the Big Gom cast, I dragged her along too. She was a great addition because not only was she beautiful but she could sing too. She and Dermot did a hilarious send up of country and western singers with songs written by Dermot with unforgettable titles such as 'The Stain on my Father's Pyjamas' and 'Don't Put the Lid on the Coffin till I Kiss Me Old Mother Goodbye'.

They also made the audience laugh with a song that was full of sexual innuendo that went something like this:
'We travelled down to Denver and up to De Moines too,
Over to St. Louis and back to Little Loo
We didn't find it there, so we moved on'.
This was sung with great pathos while both of them looked with regret at Dermot's crotch. The song was very clever as it criss-crossed all of the US and always finished with the line, 'we didn't find it there, so we moved on.'

At the end, when they had run out of place names, Marian would throw down her microphone and go over to one of the musicians and start to kiss him passionately while Dermot was left staring mournfully into his trousers.

Another important member of the cast was Deidre. I was responsible for bringing her in too as Dermot was short of 'actors'. I had met Deidre in the Italian course and we hit it off straight away. She was very pretty with beautiful, long, brown hair. Dermot always said about her that she was a genuine hippy and it was true. There was a slight Californian air about her. She was a brilliant dancer and always moved gracefully. No falling over in platform boots for her. She was the only one of us with a steady boyfriend and when they bought a house together in Bray, we all took advantage of her spare room. She helped us out by creating a boudoir atmosphere with dark-red walls, soft lamps and sultry bed linen. There was one problem with Deidre though and we all came a cropper on it at one time or another. She bought all her furniture at auction rooms and then painted it herself at home. You had to be careful when you sat on a chair in her house—I still remember the day Dermot got up from her chair with a purple arse! She dyed all the sheets too and that led to a particular incident years later. She and Paul were away and I was staying in her house for a while. My parents came to visit and stayed overnight. My mother and I were having tea in the kitchen the next morning when my father came downstairs. My mother and I gasped in shock—one side of his face was dark purple. We looked at him in horror expecting him to keel over at any minute. 'Jesus wept! He's had a stroke', my mother hissed, 'call an ambulance!'

I was about to go out to the hall to do just that when he said, in a totally, normal voice:

'God, it was very hot last night, wasn't it?'

He was perfectly fine. Looking at his face I remembered the incident with Dermot's purple arse and I ran upstairs to the bedroom where he had slept. Sure enough—purple sheets and purple pillow cases!

Poor Deidre was given the daunting task of opening the show. She was to walk out dressed as a nun. She was to sit in the middle of the stage and take out a hammer and start banging away on a piece of wood. I think Dermot was aiming for some kind of surreal, Monty Python affect and in rehearsals, we all laughed when she did it, but, of course, we never considered the fact that the audience would not get the joke. Deidre's boyfriend, Paul, was doing the lighting and he hadn't a clue what was going on either.

My sketch was the truckdriver sketch. We piled chairs up on tables to create the idea of a truck and I was the poor innocent hitch hiker who flagged down the randy truckdriver Dermot. Practically the whole sketch consisted of me trying to climb up in a tight miniskirt while wearing the infamous platform boots as the truckdriver jumped down and tried to help me up. I had to keep pulling my skirt down while slapping his hand away until I finally managed to make it up with a great leap only to fall out the other side as he had left the door open. This was pure slapstick and always got a laugh although I risked my neck every time.

The other cast members participated in the group sketches. One of these was based on a scene from the famous film 'The Godfather'. I borrowed the huge pot my mother used for boiling tea towels and we filled it with spaghetti covered in ketchup and put it in the middle of the table. Dermot sat at the head of the table doing a perfect imitation of Marlon Brando's character from the film, while the rest of us passed huge plates of spaghetti around, all the while spilling ketchup over everything. 'Brando' slapped at us randomly until suddenly a supposedly rival gang burst in carrying violin cases intending to kill us. We all dived to the floor, spilling more ketchup so that the whole scene resembled a bad splatter movie only to discover that the rival gang had taken the wrong cases and, instead of rifles, there were violins inside. It was pure chaos and more slapstick and we had only practiced it once or twice as Dermot had decided on it literally the day before the show.

Dermot had his own sketch which was a parody of Shakespeare. It was more complicated than the other sketches as it involved splitting the stage in two in order to create two different internal scenes and we needed separate curtains so that the audience could see one internal scene at a time or both together. We had help from brothers of the cast members who were more or less obliged to lend a helping hand.

The curtains on one side of the stage open and we see an Elizabethan style room. Dermot is dressed in a green tunic with ruffled collar and tights. For extra comic effect, he has stuffed a ridiculously large carrot down the front of the tights. Deidre and I were dispatched to find the perfect carrot in the vegetable market barrows on Moore Street (well-known city centre venue where street hawkers sold their wares from rickety old prams). After much searching, we had found an enormous carrot with an extra knobbly bit at the front. Dermot was delighted as his 'nob' was now an integral part of the sketch.

There was a plain wooden desk with paper and ink and a big, black phone. When the curtain opens, we see Shakespeare sitting at his desk, quill in hand, struggling over a play.

'Mackek'- he says aloud but then shakes his head.

'Mackbekon-that's it', and he begins to write enthusiastically, murmuring 'with fries or not with fries, that is the question'.

Enter servant who hands him a paper. Shakespeare stands up and starts shouting.

'No, the scurvy pox bollix hath got it wrong again'.

He picks up the phone and takes ages to dial about thirty numbers, all the while muttering to himself. The curtain closes and the other scene opens. Here we see the printer sitting at his desk with an enormous pile of handwritten sheets in front of him. He is carefully copying the title of a play and spelling out the letters: *Titus Andronicus*. He finishes and says: 'Three hundredth copies for yon candle-waster Shakespeare. May he drop dead with the pox'.

He too has a big, black phone. This phone now rings and he picks it up. The curtain on the left opens and we see Shakespeare again. He is shouting into the phone.

'Would thou wert clean enough to spit on. Thou hast got it wrong again. I said-Tight as a Duck's Arse not Titus Andronicus. Who the fuck is Titus Andronicus?

The printer looks with despair at the huge pile of hand-written sheets.

Printer: *'I wilst not change it'.*

Shakespeare: *'Vile villain, I have done thy mother'.*

The printer hangs up. The phone rings again and the printer answers in a fake female voice:

'The number thou hast dialled...'

Shakespeare is shouting again.

'Dost thy remember thine last error? Thou scribed Coriolanus instead of Curry my Anus. Thou swollen parcel of dropsies, thou stuffed cloak bag of guts'.

The printer hangs up again and the curtain closes on his side of the stage.

Now we see only Shakespeare as he strides around swearing to himself before dialling the printer again. This time he hears music playing. It is Greensleeves. The curtain on the right opens and we see the printer's studio but this time he is not present. We girls are dressed in Elizabethan costumes (somebody's awful bridesmaids' dresses) and with instruments borrowed from the music department, are supposedly playing Greensleeves. Scratchy tape recorder sounds in background. Shakespeare hangs up in disgust. Curtains close.

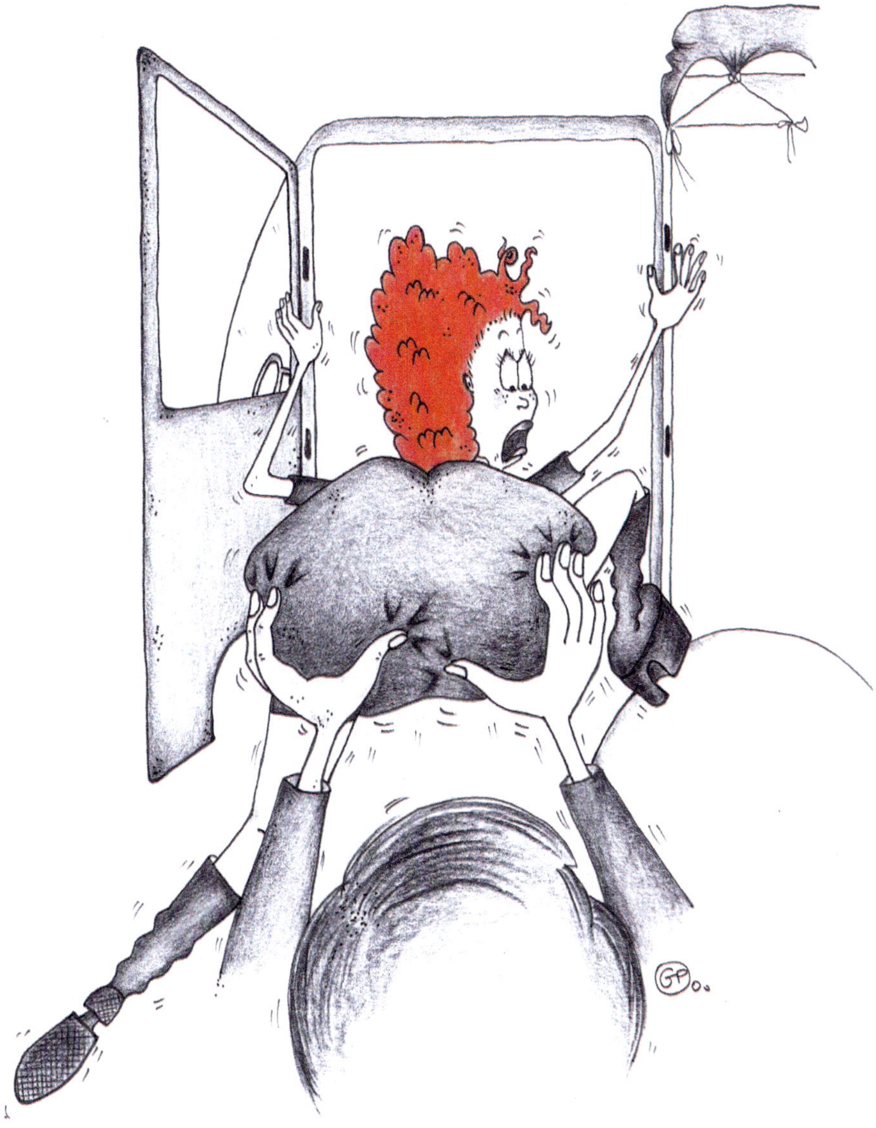

Chapter 20

How's Your Father

It was always a mistake on my part to relax in Dermot's company as he always had something up his sleeve or he simply needed to break up any kind of normal routine.

One morning he was giving me a lift to the bus stop as I was going to college and he was off on one of his forays into the world of television. We were discussing the upcoming show. I tried to explain to him the growing unease all of us felt at the thought of putting on this show without really being ready and that was an understatement. None of us had a clear idea of how it was meant to go. I could see he wasn't really listening to me, no doubt his mind was on whatever meeting he had set up. It was rush hour and there was a long line of people waiting for the bus. As we approached the bus stop and slowed down, he suddenly leaned across and opened the passenger door. He threw my bag out and started shouting at me:

'Get out, get out, you huar! How could you go to bed with three men?! You have no morals, you're a right slut.'

He shoved me out of the car.

'And one of them black', he added for good measure.

He roared off into the traffic with the passenger door swinging open. Everyone in the queue was staring at me in amazement. All I could do was fumble about in the road, stuffing everything back into my bag and then creep to the end of the queue. A little old lady in a rain mac was standing in front of me. She was wearing one of those triangular headscarves tied under her chin that old women used to wear in those days. She peered at me from under her bushy, white eyebrows and I braced myself for a sermon about how I was going to hell when she said:

'Don't mind him luv! Jaysus, shur yer only young once. My only regret is that I didn't have enough 'how's your father' [Dublin slang for sex] *when I was young. Use it or lose it I say.'*

Standing there in the bus queue, myself and Rita had an interesting conversation about how difficult it was to please *'dem men'*, as she referred to the male sex.

'Jaysus, they're never happy, they're either not gettin' enough of it or if you're wearin' yerself out for dem, they're goin' on about somthin' else. Take me advice, yer a fine-lookin' young wan, don't let any of 'em get ye up de pole, that'll be de end of ye. And don't trust dem te take precautions, dat's a laugh and a half, every babby in Ireland is born out of their precautions.'

Wise words, indeed. Rita, obviously, knew a thing or two about the average Irishman. Dermot roared laughing when I recounted this to him that evening. He always wanted to know how people had reacted to his stunts. The more shocked they were, the happier he was. But this unexpected exchange with Rita gave him an idea for a new sketch. It was to be based on that morning's incident and myself and Marian, dressed in rain macs and head scarfs, would carry on a philosophical discussion on the difficulties of dealing with *'dem men'*, to use Rita's words. Of course, we would go into more detail, talking about our lack of pleasure while we were at 'it', counting the flowers on the wallpaper, doing the shopping list in our heads and finally finishing with the line:

'Pull me nightdress down when you've finished.'

We worked on it for a few days and we all thought it was good, we imagined other people from the bus queue joining in and this time, we managed to save it when Dermot got bored with it and it did not get thrown out like most of the sketches we prepared. Both Marian and I were North-siders and could do a credible Dublin accent and it was one of the sketches that got the most laughs in the show. But this was one of the few occasions that we had the last word. We desperately needed a director but none of us had the courage to say this to Dermot.

Chapter 21

Home with the Ma

When I knew Dermot was going to be away for a few days, I usually went home to spend some time with the Ma. Despite her extreme religious views, she had a great sense of humour and I missed our chats. I had arrived one evening and we had stayed up talking till late as I told her all about the upcoming show. I gave her an abridged version as I didn't want to set her off. I didn't mention the priest sketch or the one about 'How's your father'. She wasn't convinced about the new direction my life seemed to be taking.

'Ar we goin' to be be seein' ye on the telly soon, so, what with this new actin' thing yer doin'? I don't know how 'himself' will react to that? And what about yer teachin' career? That won't go down well with de nuns.'

For once, she was right. If I had had an acting career, I could kiss goodbye to getting a teaching job as most of the schools were run by religious orders.

'Ma, don't worry, I'm never going to be an actress. I don't have any talent', I reassured her.

'Well, ye certainly ran rings around me, playin' the innocent. I never knew de half of it when it came to what ye were up to', she answered. This was a lot truer than she knew but I was happy to leave her in the dark.

'So, what is it yer doin' in this show? I know that Morgan fella is a great mimic. Shur isn't he after nearly givin' me a heart attack just the other day? I'll put manners on him the next time I see him and I'll tell ye that for nothin'.'

Here she was referring to the fact that Dermot had phoned the house a few days previously pretending to be President Éamon de Valera. Dermot had never shown any interest in politics whatsoever. He took the mickey out of them all equally. It had been during dinner in the canteen with the cast members that I had mentioned that my mother had changed her vote in the last election for the first time in her life. She had voted for Fine Gael instead of Fianna Fáil (Irish political parties). I hadn't even realised that Dermot was paying any attention to the conversation but obviously he had, as he had made this call to my poor Mam, asking her to explain the reason for her 'betrayal'. As usual, his imitation was so good that my poor mother was left speechless and had to be given tea with a good dollop of whiskey to calm her nerves afterwards. This fact reminded me that I always had to be careful around Dermot as he could multitask better than any woman.

'That fella will get himself into trouble sooner or later with his carry on.'

'You don't know the half of it, Ma', I wanted to tell her but decided against it.

'The show is just a bit of fun', I said instead. 'There's a musical part and I'm one of the back-up singers.'

'Well, he must be hard up for talent if that's the case, ye haven't a note in your head', she was quick to reply.

'Ah, Ma, that's not fair, I won that singing competition, remember?'

'I remember that there were only four of yis in it, one of them threw up from nerves, another burst out cryin' and the third didn't show up. Ye were the only one that actually sang somethin'.'

'Well, I got the medal, didn't I?'

'Ah, shur, I suppose they had to give it te someone. You were great at the Irish dancin', I'll give ye that. Ye could have gone to America to dance if yer chest hadn't grown so much'.

Here she looked straight at my boobs. *'I don't know where ye got them from. It's a shame as ye have the currels.'*

Now this was a real, sore point. I had been a talented Irish dancer and had the cups to prove it. But they were 'cups' of a different sort that ended my career. At age thirteen, I went to bed flat-chested and happy and woke up with two balloons that needed a thirty-four C bra to contain them. It broke my heart. I had to give up the dancing as I risked knocking myself out with every leap.

Having told her as much as I dared about the show, we said goodnight and went to bed. She seemed OK with the idea and I went to sleep thinking that all was right on the home front and secretly glad that she hadn't said anything about coming to see the actual performance.

I came down to the kitchen the next morning and did a double take. The contraceptive gel was lying on the table between the marmalade and the sugar bowl. The Ma's back was turned but I could feel the waves of anger coming off her. I tried to sneak back out but she'd always had eyes in the back of her head. Without turning round, she said:

'*Come back in here ye brazen hussy!*'

There was nothing for it but to face the music.

'*Is that the way I reared you?*' said she, looking at me as if I had crawled out from under a rock.

'It's not mine', said I. 'It's Deidre's.'

Deidre was my only friend who was engaged so it was a bit less sinful for her to have it.

'*And what good is it to her if you have it?* 'said she.

No flies on the Ma that's for sure.

'I was only minding it for her, I forgot to give it back.'

'*Well, get it out of this house right now! I'll get Father Mahon to do a blessing.*'

Jesus, you'd think it was radioactive by the way she went on.

Some years later, a similar scene presented itself. I came down to breakfast to find a packet of condoms sitting between the marmalade and the sugar bowl with a very red-faced, younger brother sitting at the kitchen table looking sheepish.

'*Michael has just told me that he's mindin' these for a friend*', said the Ma with lightning bolts flashing from her eyes. Then she added, giving me a dagger's look:

'Everyone in this family thinks I came down in the last shower', and with that she stalked out.

My mam and the other women in her circle all had the same attitude to sex. They considered it a burden to be borne only for the procreation of children. This was the view of the Catholic Church. If they found any pleasure in it, they were very careful to keep it hidden. I remember whispered comments between my Mam and her friends where I would glean that they were talking about IT and it was always in terms of 'he always wants IT, he never leaves the poor woman alone', or 'she had to kick him out of bed as he couldn't get enough of IT', or words to that effect. Whenever any type of lovemaking appeared on TV, even the most innocent, my Mam would be on it like a light. She'd be out of her chair and she'd have the TV off quicker than you could say 'ride me sideways'.

Chapter 22

Heathcliff

There was one thing that Dermot and I did not share and that was my passion for the west of Ireland. While I adored céile dancing and country pubs, he had time only for the siren call of RTÉ. Among my new college friends was a girl called Barbara whose brother owned a thatched cottage in Falmore in Co. Donegal. It is a place of great natural beauty but in those days, the few houses that made up the village just about managed to see RTÉ 1 if the wind was blowing in the right direction and the rabbit's ears placed on top of the TV were able to pick up the signal. The thatched cottage was my dream house with a wonderful view over the Atlantic Ocean. It didn't have running water or electricity; that didn't bother me. When I wanted to spend a weekend there Dermot would say:

'Mind you don't get run over by a cow. I'll see you when you get back.'

Getting to Falmore wasn't easy as no train or bus actually went that far and we needed to save our money for fun things so we hitchhiked. This was perfectly normal for the time as public transport outside the major cities was a joke. The roads were terrible too, narrow and bendy and you could be stuck behind a tractor for hours and it took ages to get anywhere. This was before the EEC (European Economic Community) as it was called then had granted all the money to Ireland that was used to build major highways. Back then young people holding signs with placenames were a common sight on all the roads and generally people stopped and gave them lifts.

It took about five hours to get to Falmore by car and if you were hitching it could take double that. Barbara and I used to set off from

Dublin at about eight in the morning and, depending on our luck, we would get there by early evening.

On one of these trips, we were picked up by a middle-aged man who promised to drive us to Sligo town which was a great lift for us as it was a good long distance. He was a farmer with a battered, old car with straw on the seats. All went well for the first hour or so as he asked us questions about college life but then he started to say things that set off warning bells:

'*Aren't yis too good-lookin' to be gallavantin' around the country on yer own and have yis no boyfriends to drive yis?*' This soon changed to:

'*Would ye be willing for a shilling?*' and '*would ye give me a smacker for a few bob?*'

He kept this up until we became very uncomfortable and decided that it was better to get out. This was easier said than done as he refused to stop the car. He then started to say that he was sorry and to make it up to us he would offer us some lunch in the next town we came to. Great, we thought, our chance to escape. Instead, when we got to the town and he stopped the car he refused to take our bags out of the boot so we were obliged to follow him into the hotel for tea and *sangwiches* as he pronounced it.

The tea and *sangwiches* were followed by a wee glass of sherry and then another. At this stage we were getting worried as it was late and there was no way we were going to hitch a lift in the dark. When he finally got up and went to the bathroom, we were able to take the car key and make a run for it. When I saw him coming out of the hotel, I threw the car key over the hedge and into a field so he cursing and grunting was obliged to climb over the gate and go and look for it. Fortunately, we were picked up almost immediately by a very nice woman who lived in Sligo town. She was appalled by our story and insisted that we stay the night at her house and head out again the next morning. This was a relief as we were both a bit shaken after our unfortunate episode and we settled back to enjoy the drive.

The woman's name was Kathleen which was my mother's name so I warmed to her immediately. She was extremely kind and hospitable and showed us into a lovely room where we would sleep. She went to prepare some dinner and Barbara was washing up in the bathroom when my eye was caught by someone moving outside the window. I was surprised as Kathleen had told us that she lived alone. Her house was a very nice bungalow surrounded by fields just outside Sligo town. I went to the window and looked out. I nearly jumped out of my skin when I saw someone staring back at me. To my astonishment I saw a pair of piercing, green eyes in an extraordinarily handsome face. He had long unruly, black hair and broad shoulders. When he straightened up, I saw that he was very tall. I almost fainted away. He was none other than the love of my girlish dreams, the hero of my favourite book. There in front of me was Heathcliff!

When Barbara came back from the bathroom, she could hardly understand what I was saying I was babbling so much. 'Come on', I said, dragging her to the window, 'come and see! It's Heathcliff! He exists! He's alive and well and living in Co. Sligo!' Of course, she said that I must be delirious but she soon stood gobsmacked in amazement when we went into the kitchen, and there he was putting wood on the fire. He was even more striking in the light of the kitchen and we both just stood there staring at him in awe. For his part he stared back. This intense moment was interrupted by Kathleen who came over to us and said:

'This here is Conor, he helps me out around the house. Will you have a bit of dinner with us?' she asked the vision. He nodded his head without saying anything. He went and sat down at the table.

 'Don't pay any heed to Conor', she whispered, 'he's not the full shilling.'

NOT THE FULL SHILLING! It couldn't be. Life couldn't be that cruel. I refused to believe it. Barbara went off into a fit of giggles when she saw my expression.

We sat down and started to eat. At least the others did, I couldn't swallow a mouthful. All I could do was stare at that beautiful face. He stared back.

'Now Conor, the girls will be sleeping here tonight, don't go bothering them', said Kathleen.

'Bother me! bother me!' I wanted to shout. Heathcliff did not say a word. Kathleen noticed that we were staring at each other.

'Don't be afraid of him', she said to me, 'sure he's harmless, he wouldn't touch a fly.'

'But would he touch me?', I wanted to ask. Barbara gave me a dig in the ribs.

'Stop staring at him, you'll give him ideas', she said.

'Exactly!' I answered.

'But he's retarded', she whispered.

'No, he isn't', I answered. 'He can't be!'

After dinner we helped Kathleen tidy up. Heathcliff went and sat by the fire. He still hadn't said a single word. Kathleen told me that he almost never spoke.

'He never went to school', she said, 'he can't read or write.'

Barbara was laughing again but I still wasn't willing to give up hope. I went and sat near him, ignoring Barbara who was making faces at me and snorting with laughter.

'He lives just over the hill', said Kathleen coming over to the fire. Then she turned to him and said:

'Time to go home now, Conor, see you tomorrow.' I looked at him with all the hope I could muster and for a second, I thought I saw a spark but he turned around and went out without saying a word.

We said goodnight to Kathleen and went to our room. I was totally crestfallen but still determined. I stood at the window for about an hour in the hope of seeing him but he didn't appear. Barbara was falling asleep and refused to listen to me. I had no choice but to get into bed and try to sleep.

The next morning, I woke up early and went out into the yard hoping to see my hero. I had just turned the corner of the house when I heard heavy steps behind me. I turned around and sure enough there was Heathcliff but instead of falling at my feet he was brandishing a broom at me. He literally swept me all the way back to the kitchen door, all the while muttering to himself. I was crushed. It gave a whole new meaning to the expression 'he swept her off her feet.'

This meeting with the hero of my favourite book set me thinking about how I related to men in general. I had spent years of my young life, that age when we first become aware of physical attraction, fantasising about the character of Heathcliff in 'Wuthering Heights'. Reading about him sent me into a type of sexual swoon, he was the embodiment of sexual desire as I imagined it. Of course, there are no Heathcliffs in the real world, just as there are no love stories that live on after death. It is pure fantasy and on an intellectual level, I was aware of that but it still did not account for my physical reaction to the Sligo version of my teenage fantasy. What would I have done if Conor had responded to my advances? Would I have stayed in Sligo and lived on his farm? I would like to say 'absolutely not', but I can't. And where did that leave Dermot? Did I really love him as much as I thought I did?

Once back in Dublin, I told Dermot about the Sligo episode without telling him of the sexual thrill I felt when I set eyes on Conor. But Dermot was no fool, he could sense my embarrassment although I had told him the story from the humorous point of view.

'So, basically, what you're saying is that you'd rather have a ride with a retarded farmhand than with me', was his first comment.

'Of course, not', I replied, 'I'm just saying that he looked exactly like the description in the book and it was a shame that we couldn't have a conversation.

'You could have had a version of 'Me Tarzan, you Jane' but, in this case, he could have grunted: 'Me Heathcliff, you Cathy' and you could have gone at it like rabbits', he continued.

'You've got the wrong idea, who said anything about having sex?' I asked.

'Your face did, you're scarlet.'

This was true, my face always gave me away.

However, Dermot was too sure of himself to be bothered by this fantasy of mine although he did bring it up every now and then when he wanted to see me blush.

He even considered trying out a version of a sketch on 'Wuthering Heights' for the show. He bought a black wig and put it on his head, put on a long nightshirt that he got from somewhere and had us all in stitches as he ran across the grass in UCD, holding out his arms and shouting 'Cathy! Cathy!' to the four winds. But he was making fun of me as his version of Heathcliff had more in common with *The Hunchback of Notre Dame* as he pronounced 'Sathy' instead of Cathy and staggered around, falling over his own feet.

'You see', he said to me, 'I can dribble and snivel any time you want.'

In the end, he decided not to do the sketch and this time I was glad. I didn't want to see him poke fun at what is still my favourite book but I have to admit, the sight of him in the wig and nightshirt was hilarious.

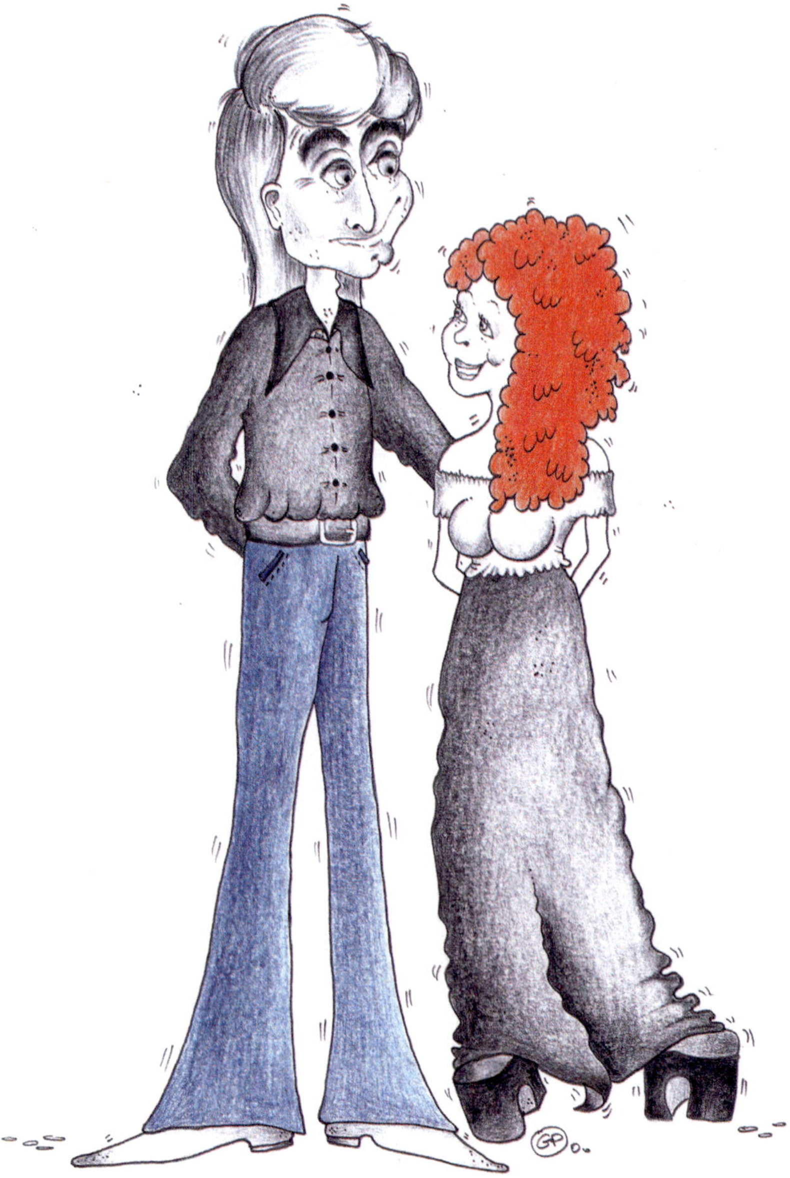

Chapter 23

Scandal

The preparations for the show were hotting up and we were all absorbed by rehearsals, which we attended religiously to the detriment of our study requirements. Dermot himself was in a frenzy of activity, always off somewhere to secure the interest of some VIP or another and we had less alone time together. I didn't complain. I understood that the Big Gom show meant everything to him and I desperately wanted it to be a success. However, my misgivings increased. I knew instinctively that we weren't ready. All I could do was hope that Dermot's genius would somehow pull it all together at the last minute. We continued in this way for those last few weeks with hardly any contact with the outside world. One weekend I felt that I really needed a break from it all and particularly from my increasing concern that it would not be all right on the night. Dermot was missing again so I decided to head home.
I was drinking tea with the Ma in the kitchen as usual. We only ever drank Barry's tea and it was always accompanied by two biscuits, usually ginger nuts, and we always had two as the Ma used to say:
'A bird never flew on one wing.'
There was a knock on the door and our Yorkshire terrier, Dougal, started to growl aggressively so we knew it was the Ma's best friend, Patty. For some reason, Dougal hated her and we would have to lock him in the downstairs loo to protect poor Patty from him. This same dog would stay religiously quiet when anyone else arrived, be they priest or tinker. We'll never understand why. Patty was one of the nicest people you could meet. 'The salt of the earth' as Dubliners say. She was wearing the ubiquitous rain mac and headscarf. She came in and sat down. The kettle was immediately put on the boil again and clean cups were produced. This particular morning Patty

was breathless and I could see that she was bursting with some news fresh off the press.

'*Wait till I tell yis, you'll never believe what I've just heard.*'

I was all ears. Patty was a great source of local gossip and I could see by her face that this was a particularly juicy one.

'*Have a cuppa first*', said the Ma, putting a steaming cup of tea in front of her, '*and a piece of apple pie*'.

'*I can't Kathleen, de doctor has me on a new diet*'.

'*Ah go on*', said the Ma, '*ye know ye want to*'.

'*Yer a divil, Kathleen, all right, just a tiny piece*'.

'*Ah shur, ye only live once. And anyways it's better to say there ye are than where are ye*', replied the Ma putting a huge slice of apple pie in front of Patty.

A strange thing about Dublin women, they never took their rain macs or scarves off if they were in someone else's house. All they would do was open the rain mac and push the headscarf back off their heads. They were always ready for flight, they always had to be home to '*get that man his dinner*', they never seemed to have any time for themselves. Patty took a sip of the tea but she was too keen to tell her news.

'*I've only just heard it meself*', she said, '*but it's all over the place already. It seems that Jackie McGowen has gone and left her husband.*'

'*What?!*' said the Ma, '*not that nice Jackie who was at school with you Livvy?*'

'*The very one*', answered Patty.

'*It seems*', she continued, '*that she's left the husband and four children and gone to live in a flat in Dublin with some young fella!*'

My mam was shocked and to be truthful, I was too. This was news indeed.

'*It seems*', Patty went on, '*that she's been carryin' on with this young fella for a while now. Eileen O'Connor saw them gettin' off the bus late one evenin' and accordin' to her they were philanderin' behind the town hall*'.

Eileen O'Connor owned the local shop and not a leaf fell in the area without her knowing. She always sat on a chair at the shop window and she would make you wait to be served if there was something interesting going on. Nothing got past her.

'*I can't believe it*', said the Ma, '*and her husband after buildin' that nice bungalow for her right next to his Mam's place.*'

This last piece of news shed some light on the matter. Maybe Jackie hadn't been so happy to go and live next door to the mother-in-law.

'*Yeah*', said Patty, '*Eileen O'Connor told me that his mother was always droppin' in some nice piece of meat or a few rashers for them*'.

'Clearer and clearer' I thought but I said nothing. Then Patty came out with a real gem.

'*And you know, I saw her in the street just the other day and I never saw her lookin' so well!*'

I spluttered with laughter and scalded myself with the hot tea. My mother and Patty both looked at me in amazement—they couldn't see what I found funny. The innocence of them! Jackie had exchanged a husband, four children and an ever-present mother-in-law for a young stud. Well, of course she was looking well.

'*There's nothin' funny about what she's done*', said the Ma, giving me one of her looks.

'*She's a disgrace to herself and her family, and an ungrateful hussy as well. It's a beautiful new bungalow.*'

I bent my head and tried to look repentant but I couldn't help grinning to myself at the thought of Jackie and her young fella in the flat far away from the bungalow and mother-in-law.

When I think of my mother and her friends now, I am struck by another fact. They all looked the same. They all had grey hair cut short, they all wore rain macs and headscarves and they all carried handbags with a packet of hard mints in them. They seemed ancient when in reality they were only in their fifties.

I was extremely glad that I wasn't living at home anymore and she no longer knew much about what I was up to.

Many years later, when I was married and living in Italy, my Italian husband and I went through a bit of a rough patch and I moved out for a few months. The Ma doted on Roberto, despite her initial misgivings about Italians with knives in their socks. For this reason, I didn't tell her about our temporary separation as I knew she would have been on his side. I only told my brother Michael as I had a different phone number and wanted him to be able to get in touch with me in case of an emergency. I swore him to secrecy and continued to call the Ma every Sunday evening as if all were normal. Then one evening I received a call from Michael which struck terror into my heart.

'You're going to get a call from the Ma, be prepared, she knows everything', he told me to my horror. 'I had no choice; she knew something was wrong and had convinced herself that one of you was dying or something. She was planning a surprise visit with Aunt Mary. I had to tell her the truth and give her your new number', Michael explained.

Of course, I understood why he had told her. The Ma was eighty-two and Aunt Mary eighty-four. To have them arrive at my old home and not find me there would have sent one or both of them to the hospital.

I hung up and waited with trepidation for the Ma's call. Sure enough, ten minutes later, the phone rang. Her first words were:

'*I believe you're in a spot of bother.*'

'Yes, Mam, it's not an easy time for me.'

'*I believe you've left your husband.*'

'Yes, but it's only…'

She didn't allow me to go on.

'*Did he hit ye?*' she asked.

'No, Ma, it's nothing…' She cut me off again.

'*Was he drinkin'?*', she asked and again I said no.

'*Was he gamblin'?*' she continued her interrogation. 'No', I answered again.

'Then he's a good husband. Mother of Sweet Incarnations, would you mind tellin' me why you went and left him?'
At last, I thought, now I'll get a chance to explain myself but I had another thing coming.
'I wasn't happy, Mam…' but I was cut off again.
'Happy? Happy? Are ye off yer trolley? Haven't ye learnt that happy and woman don't go together! Sweet Jesus, that I should have to listen to such nonsense from a grown woman. I blame dem bloody films, happy ever after my eye'!
I realized that I would never be able to explain how I felt to her but what she said next really floored me.
'Do you not realise that I've been miserable for forty years, Aunt Mary's been miserable for forty-four years and poor Patty has been miserable for more than thirty years.'
What could I possibly say to that? Patty had been miserable for less years only on account of the fact that she was a few years younger than the Ma. I gave up on my attempt to explain myself to her and she ended the call with an abrupt:
'Come back to yer senses quick or you'll have me to deal with.'
The storm blew over soon enough and I moved back home again. The Ma never spoke about it again to me except in very vague terms like: *'When ye lost the run of yerself'.*

I could never see where all the misery the Ma had spoken about came from. She ruled the roost and my Da jumped whenever she called. He was the original 'Quiet Man' and never spoke to her in any romantic kind of way. When he was ninety and in hospital, he actually said to her:
'I told you I loved you when I married you, did you expect me to be repeating myself?' This was in response to her refusing to hold his hand. The men of his generation were not affectionate, they had received little affection themselves growing up. He had been the same with us children. I had once asked my mother if dad knew our names. For all this, my mother, Aunt Mary and Patty had seemed anything but miserable to me. They were always laughing and

chatting, they went to the bingo twice a week and they certainly didn't have to deal with drunken or abusive husbands.

Chapter 24

The Show

Finally, the great day arrived. Big Gom and the Imbeciles was about to be performed. Dermot was a bag of nerves, continually changing the order of the sketches and confusing us all even more. I took him aside and tried to calm him down, but I could see he was panicking. He couldn't stay still as I was talking to him. I had to take his face in my hands and tell him to breathe deeply and listen to me.

'You have to calm down', I told him, 'and you have to stop changing the order of the sketches. We've been practising, we've got the props, you are only confusing us.'

He did calm down a bit and mercifully decided to leave the sketches in the order we had arranged.

As for the rest of us, we were all terrified. Our concern was more with letting Dermot down than making absolute fools of ourselves, such was our devotion to him.

The show was held in Theatre L, the same one where I had first seen him impersonate the head of the English department all those months ago. When I peeped out through the curtains and saw that it was packed to the rafters, I almost did a wobbly but I pulled myself together for Dermot's sake. Then he came running up to us shouting:

'Brendan Balfe's actually here! He's sitting in the front row with some of the professors. God almighty I'm fucked!'

We all rushed to assure him that we had it under control.

'Don't worry, Dermot, we've got this', I said with more courage than I felt.

One of the porters came to say that it was time to start as the crowd was getting restless and we had the lecture hall only until ten PM.

There was nothing for it but to throw ourselves over the cliff edge.

The curtains parted and the noisy crowd fell silent. Deidre, dressed as a nun but with red rubber boots, walked out onto the stage. She was carrying a hammer and a piece of wood. She told me afterwards that her legs were trembling but it didn't show. I will forever admire her courage. She took up her place centre stage and sat on the floor. She began banging on the wood with the hammer. There was a titter or two as the audience waited for something to happen, but nothing did. The crowd remained in stony silence. Behind the scenes we looked at each other in dismay. Where were the roars of laughter that we had expected? I began to feel sick. My worst fears were being realised. At this point, Dermot rallied.

'Come on, come on, get ready. Deidre will be off the stage in a minute'.

The guys who were performing in the second sketch hurriedly took up their places in the wings. Deidre came back in to some small applause and looked at me.

'I will never do anything like that again in my life', she said, 'it was a bloody nightmare'.

To our great relief, we heard the audience laughing. The guys' sketch on a mad, football trainer was going down well. We took hope. All was not lost. Marian and I got ready to go on, dressed as Rita and Phyliss. Our dialogue in a strong, Dublin accent went very well. We got lots of laughs.

The sketches continued much in the same way. Some got a lukewarm reaction, others got loud applause. I was happy with the reaction to the truckdriver's sketch as the audience roared with laughter when I fell out of the truck. I hurt my knee but I didn't care. Dermot was happy and that was all that mattered to me. His sketch on Shakespeare was a great success, the audience laughed and cheered. The last sketch was the one on the Italian mafia and it went down well too.

There was a short interval as we changed for the musical part. Dermot and Marian took their places in front of the band and I went to stand with the other two 'Tampettes'. After the first song, I

relaxed and started to enjoy myself. The audience liked the country music parody but they went wild when Dermot, after a short break, came back on dressed as Elvis in a white jumpsuit and cape. All those viewings of the Elvis documentary were put to excellent use as Dermot's impersonation was practically perfect. He had a strong singing voice and his imitation was so good that you would have been hard put to believe that he hadn't been born in Memphis. He launched into *Polk Salad Annie* and immediately the crowd was clapping and singing along. I looked at Dermot's face, he was in his element. I said a silent prayer of thanks. We were in full swing when suddenly the lights and sound system were turned off right in the middle of *Suspicious Minds*. The head porter came on and told us that we had run out of time. I couldn't believe it. The audience whistled and banged on the desks in protest, Dermot tried to convince the porter to give us another thirty minutes.
'No way', he said, 'rules are rules.'
Of course, I knew that this was due to our own lack of organisation. We should have timed everything. We could easily have omitted one or more of the second-rate sketches and made sure we could finish the musical part. Or, even more simply, we could have started on time. As it was, the ending was a fiasco. People started to file out and we were left on the stage in virtual darkness.
When we came off, Dermot went to thank Brendan Balfe for coming. I could hardly bear to look at him. His face was ashen and his jaw was clenched. None of us said anything but started to gather up our things. We had intended to go to the bar for drinks but there was no way that was going to happen now. We waited for Dermot to come back, speaking quietly among ourselves. One of the guys said that his house was empty and that we could go there.
'There's plenty of booze, no need to buy any.'
When Dermot came back, he looked exhausted and dazed. I went to him and put my arms around him.
'It was shite', he said, 'pure shite.'

'Not all of it', I answered. 'Come on, we're going to Pat's house. We can hide out there.'

We almost had to carry Dermot to the car. It was as if someone had let all the air out of him and he was flopping around with no control over his movements. When we were safely inside the empty house, we all made a determined effort to raise his spirits, but it was useless. We looked at each other helplessly, we didn't know how to console him.

'Drink! Lots of drink! That's what we need', said Pat, the first to come out of our frozen state.

'Yes', we all shouted, 'we need drink!', and so it was. Bottles were opened and passed around; we didn't bother with glasses. I kept my eyes glued to Dermot. He didn't touch a drop. At a certain point, he got up and went outside. I followed him. He was leaning on the wall outside, staring into the darkness.

'I touched his arm. 'Come back inside', I said gently.

He didn't answer me. He just kept staring into space. I went back inside.

By this time, the others had revived a bit. They were telling themselves that it had gone quite well and that it was all the porter's fault.

Marian came up to me and asked where Dermot was. 'He's outside', I told her.

'Go to him', she said to me.

I wanted to, more than anything, but I couldn't. The depth of his despair frightened me. I didn't know how to comfort him. I was always in difficulty when faced with these extreme moods of his. I was aware that I didn't have the means to deal with them. I felt helpless when confronted with it on this occasion. Looking back, I greatly regret not having gone to him, not having held him, I feel that I let him down when he needed me most.

We stayed the night in Pat's house, sleeping on the sofas and on the floor. We didn't go upstairs to the bedrooms; we needed the presence of the others for comfort. I went outside to check on Dermot but he wasn't there. His car was gone too. With a heavy heart I went back inside and curled up on the sofa beside Marian. She gave me a blanket and I wrapped myself tightly in it. I lay there in the dark unable to sleep. The hours passed slowly. It was a relief when I saw the first light of dawn creep through the curtains. I went into the kitchen and made some tea, as little by little the others began to stir. None of us were in the mood for talking as we thanked Pat and took our leave. What a difference this weary band of stragglers was to the nervous but excited group we had been just the evening before. There was no sign of Dermot and we were lost without him.

Chapter 25

The Aftermath

In the following days we began to hear the reviews of the show, mainly from other students and the people who wrote for the college review. It had not been the disaster we had feared although the general consensus was that it had not been up to the standard of previous *Big Gom* shows. The musical part with Dermot as Elvis had been much appreciated and we even took a fuller version of this on the road. We all piled into a creaky old van belonging to someone's uncle and travelled to various school gyms and parish halls to play before enthusiastic audiences of young and old. The magic of Elvis crossed the generation gap and the crowd loved us. We could have done more with this but Dermot's heart wasn't in it and he soon lost interest.

On a personal level, my relationship with Dermot ended on the night of the show. In today's terms, we would say that he 'ghosted' me. He stopped seeking me out and we no longer spent any alone time together. We never had a proper break-up, just as we had never been a proper couple. I felt guilty for abandoning him on the night after the show and I accepted his departure from my life as a consequence of that. On another level however, I also realised that Dermot had done what he always did. He moved on. I say this without any bitterness. I had had no illusions whatsoever regarding his feelings for me.

But all the colour had gone out of life for me. It was May and the weather was warm and sunny. The students were lying on the grass and studying in groups outside, chatting and laughing together. I did not join them; I found the sun hurt my eyes and the sound of their laughter was painful to my ears. I preferred the quiet gloom of the library. The final exams were looming and I had lots of work to catch up on which was a Godsend as I didn't have much time for moping. I attended lectures, slipping out just before the end to avoid any contact, preferring to study alone.

Our band of brothers also broke up for what is a cult without its leader. Dermot was nowhere to be seen and the group drifted apart. Only we three girls stayed in touch. I remained close friends with Marian and Deidre but I lost contact with the boys. Deidre had her life with Paul, whom she married soon afterwards.

Marian finally got me out of the blues by suggesting that we go to the U.S. to work for the summer months. We got a visa and booked a flight to San Francisco. The idea of going to Hippy Heaven galvanised me. I threw myself into my studies and started counting the days to the end of term.

The day the plane took off from Dublin airport on the seventeen-hour flight to San Francisco I started to feel like my old self again. I looked out the window at the green fields of home and rejoiced in the fact that I would not be seeing them again for four months.

Epilogue

I came out of my reverie to the awful reality of the nightmare that surrounded me. As Italy had been the first country in Europe to be affected by the Covid virus, we were hit the hardest as we had had no time to prepare. We were in strict lockdown and I felt terribly isolated. Although I have lived in Italy for most of my adult life, I still consider Ireland 'home' and have always gone back frequently. My true friends are my Irish ones, the Fab Four from school and Deidre from college. The lockdown restrictions made it impossible for me to make my twice-yearly visits and this added greatly to my sense of aloneness.

Having gone down memory lane and relived such a happy time, I had no desire to return to the dreadful present. I decided to concentrate on those wonderful memories and use them as a blessed escape from what was going on all around me. I wrote to old friends, asking them what they remembered and I noted their memories down. I began to fill a notebook which soon became a copybook. I discovered that the more I remembered, the clearer the past came back to me. Writing down my memories of that wonderful year spent with Dermot helped me to get through the worst days of the lockdown. I will always be grateful to him for that.

One of my worst memories is of the terrible day that I heard of Dermot's death. As it happened, I was in Ireland at the time and it was announced at the start of the one o'clock news on the car radio. It came as such a dreadful shock. I had been following Dermot's career with great interest and was a huge fan of the *Father Ted* tv series. I was able to watch it as my beloved mam taped all the shows for me and sent them over so I would have a *Father Ted* marathon long before such a thing became popular. The news was very hard to take in as Dermot had always been such a force of nature. I couldn't believe that he was gone.

Dublin city may well be a sprawling metropolis but its centre is more akin to a country town where you can just bump into people. Over the years I had met Dermot a few times by chance, usually in Grafton Street, and we always had a drink and a chat. It was wonderful to meet him, he would have me falling off my chair laughing just as in the good old days. He would tell me about his life, happy times during the *Scrap Saturday* period although I had been away from Ireland for so long, I wasn't able to fully appreciate the satire. I had met him in one of his darker times when RTE had axed his show and he was bitingly critical of them. My heart bled as I could see how painful this disappointment was for him. Then there were good times again and he would be his usual mischievous self. On our last meeting, many years before *Father Ted*, he took me to dinner in Howth and we laughed as we remembered our failed attempt to gate-crash Gay Byrne's party. He was in high spirits; things were going well for him. As he was about to drive me home, he winked at me and said:

'I suppose a ride would be out of the question?'.

Chapters

Prologue 7
The Letter 9
The Outfit 12
The Encounter 15
Library 19
The Culchie in the Bus 22
The Big Gom Cast 25
The Priest's Walk 27
A Fling 31
Contraceptives 36
A Perfect Day 38
Lying to the Ma 40
Phone Messages 45
The Loony on the Bus 47
Going Out with Elvis 54
The Priest in the Pub 56
The Coffee Dock 59
Housemates 65
Gate-crashing 67
The Cast Part II 72
How's Your Father 80
Home with the Ma 82
Heathcliff 86
Scandal 93
The Show 99
The Aftermath 104
Epilogue 106

Printed in Great Britain
by Amazon